D1808699

Kiss Yourself Goodbye

KISS YOURSELF GOODBYE

A Matt Sinclair Mystery

Tony Fennelly

Arlington Books
King St, St James's
London

KISS YOURSELF GOODBYE
First published 1989 by
Arlington Books (Publishers) Ltd
15-17 King Street, St James's
London SW1

© Tony Fennelly 1989

'A House Is Not a Home' – Words by Hal David
Music by Burt Bacharach
© Diplomat Music Corp
Lyric reproduced by permission of Famous Chappell

British Library Cataloguing-in-Publication Data

Fennelly, Tony
Kiss yourself goodbye.
I.   Title
813' .54 [F]

ISBN 085140–767–6

Typeset by TJB Photosetting Ltd, Grantham, Lincs
Printed and Bound in Great Britain by
Billing & Sons Ltd, Worcester

For Louise Ihde Ulan

Who has borne, uncomplaining
the ignominy of being my best friend.

PROLOGUE

Saturday Afternoon

Rodger Lloyd had four minutes to live.

The distinguished political consultant held up a bottle of Pernod then shook his head and chuckled.

"No. Of course you wouldn't drink. But you don't mind if I have one? I'm a little nervous, but now you understand why this evening was so important."

Rodger Lloyd was elegantly dressed for his last day of life in an Oxford wool chalkstripe of a weight appropriate for his home in Chicago but perhaps too warm for New Orleans in October.

He turned his back on his visitor and reached for the glass neatly paper-bagged by the French Quarter hotel. Then he had just enough time to pour his brandy and put it to his lips, but not to taste it before the seven-inch fishing knife was plunged between his shoulder blades, ripping through his lungs.

Rodger Lloyd's murderer watched him pitch forward, letting his glass fall and bounce and roll while he groped at the air above him with both hands. The murdered toppled full-length across the rug, landing with a dull thud, and the murderer knelt to assure that the wound was a fatal one before calmly walking out of the hotel room and down the corridor to join a cluster of tourists awaiting the elevator.

A second after the door closed. Rodger Lloyd struggled to his knees. His fine mind being at its very sharpest in this last minute before extinguishment, he calculated that he had just blood and breath enough to take him to his book of Audubon plates on the bed table. Clawing desperately at the pages, he had barely the strength left to turn to the right color plate and then to rest his head on the open volume to die. Because he knew who had murdered him.

He was never to know why.

CHAPTER ONE

Monday Evening

"A *nose* job!"

Steve Hicks, my second-in-command, tapped his supermarket tabloid. "Cher went out and got herself a *nose* job! Gospel in Midnight. Do you believe it?"

Steve was supposed to be observing our usual Monday night ritual of adding invoices. But so compelling a national issue as a celebrity's nose would distract even the most diligent.

He paused, calculator, in hand, to await my comment. "Well?"

"Poor Cher is a knife-junkie," I said. "Do you have the sales tax totals?"

"Don't get me wrong, Matt. It's not that I have anything against medical science." He passed me his legal pad with sums double-checked. "After all, I didn't mind her getting the teeth bonded. They were a genuine flaw. And then when she had that breast-lift..."

"Twice."

"Twice. Well, I still didn't get mad. Guess I figured that was none of my business."

"Right—Where is the invoice for the Colonial bedroom suite?"

"Under your left elbow—But then she has to go out and get this *nose* job. I mean she was beautiful before!"

"I agree—We've already got three orders for that Queen Anne sofa. Custom upholstered, naturally."

"See, Cher was a classic! She had this regal Cleopatra nose. A Nefertiti nose. And now she's got...What?"

"What?"

"Some kind of *Heather Locklear* nose. A *Connie Selleca* nose!"

"A some-cute-flight-attendant-named-Bambi nose."

"Exactly." He punched the air. "And then like that wasn't *enough* to deal with, today the goddamn stock market has to go and drop five hundred and eight friggin' points!"

"If it's not one thing, it's another—Toss me the calculator."

Steve flipped it onto my desk blotter then leaned back in his swivel chair, creaked, and stretched.

"Say, Matt. Maybe we're just making extra work for ourselves here. Seeing as everyone in the market is twenty percent poorer tonight, our customers might be calling in to cancel some of these orders."

"Fear not. New Orleans has been depressed for years, but our customers always have money.

The oil bust has closed down a vital portion of Louisiana's coastal industry. And the general recession has cut into the region's tourist business like nobody's business. The local newscasters drone of double-digit unemployment. The welfare rolls are swollen to bursting, and former pipe-line welders who used to make fifteen hundred a week now hang around outside Schwegmann's and offer to watch your car for a quarter. At least they have an enterprise.

In this era of Reaganomics, people have less, spend less, try to fix up the old goods and forego the new.

New Orleans department stores are closing their Canal Street locations and moving out to the malls where the white people live. Those teachers, accountants and civil servants who still get paychecks.

But my shop, New Traditions, will remain secure here in its little corner of the Vieux Carré. Mine is a recession-proof business because we've always catered to what they used to call "the carriage trade". Our premium-quality antique reproductions are very expensive, but our clients are very rich. Rich people stay that way in good times and bad.

When a local manufacturer feels an economic pinch, he may close down a plant and lay off three hundred employees. But he won't deny his wife a new Caffieri-style secretary with ormolu mounts, marquetry and intarsia. And she'll come to me for it.

Steve had exhausted the subject of Cher's nose and had broached the feasibiltiy of a hair transplant for "that guy on Moonlighting" when the office phone jangled a welcome interruption. It was after business hours, so I just answered, "Matt Sinclair".

"Matty? This is Sylvia."

Sylvia was the ditsy wife of my first cousin George Sinclair. And she had never in her life said anything remotely interesting.

"Hello dear."

I dropped the phone on my desk speaker so I could grunt and sort invoices at the same time.

"Gosh, I hate to bother you, but…"

Then the anxiety in her voice registered and I had a second of panic. "But what? Anything wrong?"

I meant, "Did something happen to Pip? Did he try too high a jump and fall into a fence?!"

"I'm not sure." Now Sylvia's voice became reassuringly dithery like the rest of Sylvia. "The police say I should talk to a lawyer."

No crisis with my favorite nephew. I resumed sorting.

"I'll recommend a good one if you like. You know I don't practice anymore."

"But another lawyer would charge me something. Wouldn't he?"

"Undoubtedly. What's the problem?"

"Lieutenant Washington thinks I may be… Now this is weird…"

"What's weird?" I was alerted again. Frank Washington was with NOPD Homicide.

"Sort of implicated in a murder."

I dropped my papers in a heap. "You?!"

"Isn't it weird?"

"No. Have you been charged with anything?"

"Well the lieutenant didn't come right out and accuse me yet, but…"

"Where are you calling from?"

"I'm here at home."

"Stay put and don't say 'Tchwenk'. I'll be right over." I disconnected and reached for my coat.

"Steve, you'll have to solo tonight. I'm needed elsewhere."

"You're..?" He didn't have to ask for instructions as he moved over to my chair, nor I to give any. Steve has worked for me these eight years and needs no supervision. He could probably run New Traditions by himself for a month at a time.

With all his industry though, Steve Hicks still doesn't have that special *Je ne sais quoi* necessary to make one of two dozen French Quarter furniture stores a unique and high-profit operation. He's heterosexual.

I sprinted through the dim showroom and let myself out onto Royal where the street lamps were just blinking on and tourists in rude T-shirts swung their shopping bags and walked sideways, gawping up at the ironwork balconies. I bobbed and weaved through the flocks of them, jostling one another and apologizing in nasal yankee accents.

It was a brisk six blocks back to my house where I keep the car. There being no such thing as parking in the Quarter. I walked fast and drove fast.

My first cousin George and I had almost nothing in common but our surname. However his family was the only posterity I had.

Sylvia and George lived their lives of quiet desperation in a paint-chipped blue-collar neighborhood on Banks Street, south of Canal. The lawns down there are cut, not manicured. The cars out front aren't new and expensive, but they're not up on blocks either.

As I nosed my burgundy SEL 500 curbside, I caught a glimpse of blinds and draperies being drawn apart behind smudgy windows. A Mercedes was a rarity in this part of town. So, for that mattter, was a Sinclair.

In our parents' generation, the Depression had ravaged the economy and the family coffers. So by 1935 there was nothing left to the Sinclair name but the name itself, two handsome brothers, and a rickety old mansion of St. Charles Ave.. Fortunately my father, Arthur, was tall, dashing, and the best ballroom dancer on the Delta. So he did what Sinclairs do when they have no money. He married some. Clèmentine Vigé was not tall or beautiful but the match was optimum. My mother is the smartest woman in the world at this writing.

Arthur's younger brother, James Lane, was misguided enough to marry for passion. The bride was from the Irish Channel and had a prodigious figure, but no other criteria of a traditional Sinclair wife.

James Lane Sinclair was killed in an accident in 'fifty-two, leaving his widow and three year old son penniless.

Now the son, my first cousin George, was thirty-eight years old and still penniless. He taught Industrial Arts at McDonogh High School for a cool twenty-two thousand a year.

I parked on the street because it had rained a "goose drowner" each of the last three mornings and the dirt and shell driveway was now axel-deep mud. Ahead of me, Frank Washington's car had also found high ground. It was unmarked but easily spotted as an LTD Crown Victoria, the same model year as most other police cars in the city.

Sylvia had opened the door before I crossed the front porch, the October wind blowing her muslin granny dress, discolored with food stains.

George's bad taste in women may have exceeded even his father's. My cousin married Sylvia back in the late sixties when he was a peacenik facing the draft and she a long-haired flower child festooned with love-beads. Now she still lived there: back in the late sixties. Her mind having been softened by psychedelic drugs, Sylvia still wore tie-dyed T-shirts, and sang Joan Baez songs off-key.

Her hair was still uncut and plaited as it had been for twenty years. The ragged tip of her braid was a dull black which faded halfway up to a drab gray.

But I had to love her in spite of all her flaws because she gave me my nephew Philip. Brilliant, charming and handsome, the boy brightened a room just by entering it. Sylvia's mantlepiece was laden with his athletic trophies and honors awards from St. Boniface High School, and those of his brother Ronald.

"Oh Matt, thank you for coming! This is all so..." At a salient look from me, she choked off the "weird" and turned to her visitor in the double parlor behind her. "Do you know Frank Washington?"

"All too well." I walked past her to shake his hand. Frank is a large, imposing man, physically well-suited to his vocation. He was one of the first blacks to be made lieutenant in his precinct and remains that other, even rarer, entity: an honest cop. "Nearly fifteen years, since my salad days with the D.A.'s office."

"Way back when you still had ideals." Frank considered the occasion too grave for a smile. But he twitched his mustache to indicate that he would have performed one under other circumstances.

Sylvia fluttered her hands in turquoise squash blossom bracelets. "This is all because I had a friend back in college." (I surmised that a polygraph would have measured a galvanized response at the term "friend".) "And he had this terrible accident Saturday."

"Accident? I think he was murdered on purpose," Frank offered sourly. He had armed himself with the Times-Picayune folded to page three and handed it to me now. "Did you read about the late Rodger Lloyd?"

"That campaign manager from Chicago? I caught Margaret's report on Channel Eight."

I hadn't taken much note of the event, even though it had occurred in a Bourbon Street Hotel only eight blocks from my house on Esplanade. Violence is rampant in New Orleans: drug-related, mob-related, sex-related,...Or simply the kill-a-man-to-make-it-easier-to-get-his-watch-off variety.

Frank Washington said, "This was no ordinary mugging, Matt. This victim wasn't robbed. No drugs were involved, and he wasn't a homosexual."

"In which case it would have served him right."

"In which case he might have invited some unsavory local

character up to his room and been vulnerable to any atrocity the character wanted to visit on him."

"Like your typical American fag-bashing."

"But it wasn't. Nor did it fit any of the other stranger-murder profiles. He was killed with a fish-gutting knife."

"Was he a fisherman?"

"No, it seems he was a birdwatcher." Frank couldn't help twitching at that news. "The fatal weapon was probably not Lloyd's own, so someone must have brought it up to the room."

"Indicating that the attack was premeditated."

"Now you're beginning to get it. We suspect this was not a random murder but personal."

I skimmed the three-column article whose file photograph showed a fair and handsome Rodger Lloyd. "Who would want to kill a campaign manager?"

"Maybe you can tell me, Matt." Frank raised an eyebrow, just one, which I wish to hell I could do. But mine don't work independently.

I tried anyway but both went up. "How do you mean?"

"Aren't you heavily involved with the Mayor's primary?"

"Only because Armand Voitier is my third cousin."

Like most campaigns in recent years, we had three shades of candidates to choose among: Farley Berber, a red-neck white man, on the political right, a black man named Moses Jones with a heroic civil rights record on the left, and somewhere in between, a moderate of mixed blood. My cousin Armand.

"But I don't make policy for his campaign," I told Frank.

"Did you know Rodger Lloyd?"

"Only what I read in Newsweek."

"Then he wasn't hired to work for Voitier."

I handed back the newspaper. "Armand's campaign is managed by his law partner, Edward Stokes."

He glanced at the picture on page three. "We don't suspect a political connection at this point, but we have to cover every contingency."

I share your sense of tragedy about the event. But what does any of it have to do with Sylvia? Just because she and Lloyd were..uh.. 'friends back in college?"

Sylvia twisted her wedding ring around her finger. "I guess it's because I was the last one to go to Rodger's room."

Here was another surprise. Lloyd was only a second-rank political consultant but his millieu was still a bit rarefied for a plain hausfrau like Sylvia. Even if they'd been college sweethearts, why would he look her up after all these years?

Were she a part of my past, I should prefer to leave her there.

"Mrs. Sinclair hasn't denied that circumstance either," Frank averred.

"Well.., I did go up there," she volunteered like a loon.

"Stow it, Sylvia. Don't say another word on advice of your attorney." I turned to Frank. "You tell me how you brought her into this."

He folded his arms and closed his eyes as though reciting by rote. "We went over the scene of the crime according to procedure and combed every square inch. We found a piece of scrap paper in the victim's pocket on which he had written one local phone number. It was Mrs. Sinclair's."

"That's trivial and coincidental. You storm in here and use the weight of the law to frighten this poor woman on the evidence of a jotted phone number?"

"Wait, there's more." Frank opened his eyes and pulled out his ubiquitous note pad. The mustache twitched again. "At one o'clock, Mrs. Sinclair asked a desk clerk named Jasper Mars for Mr. Lloyd's room number."

Sylvia tugged at her soiled frock, trying to pull out a wrinkle. "Rodger told me the room number and I wrote it down on a Kleenex, but then I blew my nose and.." I shot her a look that would shrivel a squid and she shut up.

Frank resumed. "At two o'clock, Mr. Lloyd was found dead. And here's something else I would like to share with you, Matt." He reached into his coat pocket and handed me a folder of 5″ by 7″ glossies.

They weren't publicity pictures.

"Do I have to?"

"You'd better."

I scanned the exhibits with the worst of wills. "Excellent color reproduction. So Mr. Lloyd got stabbed in the back and left a bodacious amount of blood all over the rug."

"Right." Frank nodded. "Why?"

"Why?"

He reached over and pointed. "Blood all over the rug because the victim moved after he was stabbed, as you can see."

"All right, he tried to crawl for help."

"Open your eyes, Matt. The trail shows that Lloyd was killed over by the dresser. The phone was to his right, but he headed in the opposite direction to the bed table. He wanted that book of Audubon plates."

"He couldn't have expected to read it."

"Not likely."

"So what do we have here? A 'dying message'?"

"Right out of Ellery Queen? Could be." Frank produced a magnifying glass from his breast pocket. "And if you'll look closely you can just barely see that he died with his head right on the plate of the Garden Warbler."

I have excellent vision, but still I needed his lens.

"Yes, I see it now: the Garden Warbler. So what? Does that mean something to you?"

"Not to me. But to an ornithologist like Lloyd, it means 'Sylvia Borin'. That's the Latin name."

"And you think Lloyd wanted to indicate that he was murdered by someone named.. Sylvia?"

"Add the fact that Mrs. Sinclair has admitted to being the only person in town Lloyd knew by that name."

"Never admit anything, Sylvia." Then I assumed a tone at once reasonable and condescending. "Now, how could she possibly know of all the man's acquaintances?"

At that, the moss-head had to step forward, wringing fleshy hands. "Well, I was sure because he'd only been in town, like, four days, and.." She would have dithered herself right into the electric chair. I put a hand over her mouth and continued in my best summation voice.

"Listen, Frank, you've got nothing for indictment here. Even if you accept this 'dying message' angle, Lloyd might have been pointing to someone named 'Bird'. Or a feather-weight boxer. Or even a book-maker."

"No sale. If you'll notice, those pages to his right are bloody and wrinkled as though he had turned them to get to that particular plate."

"Maybe you're looking at it wrong. What's there on the facing page?"

"'Fraid you can't do much with that. It's Cuculus canorus: the common cuckoo."

Sylvia chewed her plait. "Do we know anyone named 'Cuckoo', Matty?"

"Maybe we do." I set my mouth on automatic and ran it. "Or possibly a mental patient. Or Lloyd might have been pointing to some German from the Black Forest. Or a Swiss clock-maker. That so-called 'dying message' isn't even circumstantial evidence. And then, where's your motive?"

"I knew you would come up with all that jazz. So would any defense lawyer." The lieutenant sighed and put away his note book. "We couldn't go to the D.A. with this for evidence, but Lloyd just might have been telling us where to look. They haven't analyzed all the hair and fiber samples yet. —Like to walk me to my car?"

"It would be an honor."

We left Sylvia staring down at her murky rug and negotiated the muddy walkway out to his unit. The radio was quiet.

I found some dry footing and leaned against his fender.

"Now what can you tell me about Rodger Lloyd?"

He shrugged. "White male cauc, six feet-two, blond and blue, forty-seven years old.."

"Not the dry stats."

"Okay, he was famous in political circles as an 'image doctor'."

"You mean he would tell candidates how to sell themselves to the greatest number of voters."

"Exactly. And here we are right in the middle of the biggest, hottest, most expensive mayor's campaign in New Orleans history. One of the three candidates might have called him in for the primary."

"Or he might be here as a tourist."

"Yeah? So might I." Frank opened the car door and settled his burly frame behind the wheel. Say, Matt. I'm sure your cousin is unaware that she's growing illegal plants in her window box. I didn't see it this time."

He pulled out onto Banks Street where he weaved from side to side, carefully avoiding potholes so as not to damage Parish property.

CHAPTER TWO

Monday Evening

I sloshed back into the house to confer with my client.

"Oh, Matt! Thanks for coming over right away. I was wigged out with George staying late at school. I didn't know who to call.

"I was the one to call."

She led me into her dingy kitchen and brushed dried crumbs off the formica table.

"I wasn't expecting company today or I'd have cleared a place."

She rested an elbow on the latest *Cosmoplitan* and proferred a melmac plate of chocolate chip cookies.

I accepted one in lieu of retainer. "All right, now that the law has gone, you can tell me, and only me, *everything*."

"You'll handle my case then?"

The retainer was hard, flat, and greasy. Too much shortening. "I hope it won't need handling. What about your relationship with the victim? When did you first meet Rodger Lloyd?"

"Back in the early seventies. I was majoring in Sociology at Newcomb and Rodger was, like, an adjunct prof at Tulane."

"You were close friends?"

"Well,.." She stared at the oven. "This is hard to say.."

"I'm not *People Magazine*. Let's just stipulate that you had an intimate relationship."

"Yeah, okay." She switched her stare over to the washing machine. "But it was heavier than that, you dig? I was already married to George. But he was in Vietnam for two years."

"I remember. So during your husband's tour overseas, you were having an affair with the deceased."

"I couldn't help it."

"I don't care if you could help it."

"It was, like, Karmic destiny." She tried to make me take another cookie but I dodged. "Rodger was a very exciting lecturer and every chick in the class was zonked over him. But he would speak directly to me, sort of holding me with his eyes, you dig? And we just naturally grooved together."

"I'm not your confessor."

"Well, I aced the course."

"Irrelevant. Had you kept in touch with Lloyd over the years?"

"No way." She seemed to come out of her torper and faced me squarely. "He blew town soon after and I never heard from him until this week."

"Great. So we'll just point out that you couldn't possibly have had any motive to murder a man, even an ex-lover, after all this time."

"Yeah, but.. it was a bad scene."

"It usually is."

She fingered her plait. "I thought we had something, like, existential together but he just up and split."

"Until a few days ago."

"Right. So then he just wafts back down here expecting to groove again."

"I don't get it." (I didn't.) "Do you think Rodger Lloyd still loved you?"

She looked startled at the very notion. "Me? No way. He just wanted to screw everything up."

"Were you afraid he would tell your husband about the affair?"

"George was already hip." She gave her attention back to the washing machine. "When Ronald was six and Phillip was five, I got into one of my depression scenes. That's when I swallowed all those downs and had to go to Pineville."

"Nearly ten years ago. I remember."

Pineville is Louisiana's state mental facility. Sylvia had been diagnosed a case of "toxic psychosis" and carried off in a straight jacket. We all thought she might be consigned to live out her wretched life on Thorazine, weaving baskets and shuffling around in carpet slippers. But she was released to her husband's care within the month.

"My therapist there said I was heavy into this guilt trip and I should cop to George about Rodger. So the next visiting day, I spilled the whole story."

"Then George knows about you and Lloyd."

She nodded dully. "I had to tell him."

"Was confession good for the soul?"

"Maybe." She sighed and slumped over. "I was sprung two weeks later, after they shot some more electricity into my gourd. But it wasn't too groovy for our relationship." She heaved herself out of her chair and trudged to the stove. "I got the feeling there are some things a chick should keep to herself."

"Amen." I myself only confess when it doesn't matter.

"Are you into coffee? I have Maxwell House Instant."

"No thank you."

"I make it according to the recipe. I always bring it to a boil first just like the gourmet chefs."

"So how did Lloyd come back into your life?"

"I read in Betty's column that Rodger would be in town, but I never dreamed he'd want to see me again. It seemed so final back in.." Sylvia tried to pour her hot brown liquid into a "World's Greatest Mom" mug but her hand shook. "Anyway, it was easy for him to find me. My name hasn't changed in all those years and we're in the book." She added a shovel-load of sugar to the mixture and returned to the table. "He came by last Wednesday when no one else was home. He sat right in that chair and I offered him Kool-Aid and a Pudding Pop."

"Of course."

"But he didn't want them."

"No?"

"He must have just eaten. Then he told me what he'd been up to all those years."

"Hold on, Sylvia. Something here doesn't compute. If you had already told your husband, how could Lloyd make trouble for you?"

Sylvia ducked her head like a turtle retreating into its shell. "He was bad news. That's all."

She was hiding something and that was stupid. I approached from another direction. "Tell me everything that happened Saturday."

"I remember it rained hard that morning. So I just wrote him a letter asking him to stay out of my face." She used the issue of Cosmo for a place mat, her coffee mug making a wet brown ring on the cover portrait of Paulina. "But by ten, the sun was out, so I put the letter in my purse and hopped a bus to Rodger's hotel to deliver it personally. I thought I'd appeal to his inner soul."

"You spoke to him?"

"No way, José. I knocked on his door and shouted but there was no answer. Then I tried to push the letter under the door but the rug was too thick. So I just dropped it back in my purse and split."

"You asked the desk clerk for his room number. Did you talk to anyone else on the way out?"

"No, I was too spaced. But I didn't know Rodger was going to be croaked. How could I know that?"

"Then you returned home?"

"Nah, there was nothing to do here. Phillip gives riding lessons Saturdays, you know. And Ronald is kind of a drag because he's always making with his computer. George was out fishing, natch. He gets into his pick-up truck and goes fishing every weekend. That's his bag."

"If not home, where did you go?"

She put her head down to sip the coffee. "Just bopped on up to the River Walk. I tried to get the Rodger thing out of my skull by trucking through the little shops."

"I'd like some corroboration. Would anyone have seen you?"

"On Saturday afternoon, the mall was really shaking. I don't think anyone noticed me."

Understandable. I wouldn't have noticed her if we'd been together in a phone booth. "Did you buy anything?"

"Who can afford to buy? I'm a shop teacher's wife. No, I just came home and fixed a tuna cassarole. Then everyone blew in at the usual time to eat."

I leaned over and pulled the limp curtain aside. Just as Frank said, there was a splendid bloom of Cannibis Sativa in the window box. "Get rid of this."

She blinked. "But Matt, that's my relaxation."

"Grow African Violets. The police are bound to show up again and they won't all be as charitibly near-sighted as Frank Washington."

We heard the front door open and shut and Sylvia lifted her head one bare inch. "The boys are home from school."

I had more enthusiasm than she and sprung up to meet him. Them. I couldn't help breaking into a grin at the sight of Philip. Due to natural circumstances, I would never beget children of my own, so once removed would have to do. My cousin's younger son, "Pip", though not technically my nephew was close enough in blood to be my emissary to the future and my agent of immortality.

Fortunately, Pip met every hope and expectation for an heir.

Pip was a year younger than his brother Ronald but already stood three inches taller, and was fair and handsome like a true Sinclair. Poor Ronald, by contrast, took after his mother which made him short and stocky with poor vision corrected by thick glasses. Very un-Sinclair. The men in my family have eagle eyes. Not one in my line of ascent has ever needed glasses.

"Uncle!" Pip leapt and hugged me. "Are you here to take me for a driving lesson?" He was studying for his license and I had volunteered to take him out.

"No, but I'll pick you up at the stables tomorrow night."

Ronald hung back and nodded at me with grave courtesy.

"Good evening, Uncle Matt." No more than that was needed from him and so he repaired to his room to play with his computer.

Sylvia walked me out the door and across the porch where

we wouldn't be overheard. "Thanks for talking to the Lieutenant. You don't think he really suspects me, do you?"

"No," I said, meaning "Not yet."

The wind was coming up and she hugged herself.

"Cripe. What am I gonna do about George?"

"George?"

"He'll be royally pissed."

CHAPTER THREE
Tuesday Morning

"Sure you don't want breakfast?"

Robin held up the skillet to illustrate that he was both willing and prepared to accommodate.

"No thanks, kitten, just coffee. Turn on the news."

As Robin stepped to the buffet and flipped on the T.V., I opened my bottles of vitamins and minerals and lined up the pills according to size and color. For every year I get older, that much greater becomes the number and variety of diet supplements: Choline for the brain, vitamin B complex for the skin, iron for the blood, selenium for the hair, dolomite for the bones, and then, of course, there's the zinc.

I'm somewhat furtive about the zinc.

Robin poured my coffee then measured in the prescribed amounts of sugar and milk in an attempt to be useful now that we were again between maids. I had owned the Queen Anne style house some thirteen years and assorted broom-leaners had come and gone at the rate of one every two months. There was only our ground floor apartment to clean, the second and third stories being given over to tenants. The work wasn't too hard and the pay was fair. But, alas, there's no honorable servant class anymore. That stratum having long been replaced by the welfare class.

Robin spilled some of the sugar and tiny white grains bounced and sparkled on the damask. My little nit wasn't much of a housekeeper but then I hadn't chosen him for utilitarian purposes.

I asked, "Did you find my old work clothes?"

"Way in the bottom of the trunk. Those things are all yicky with oil and grease."

"Things get that way on a pipe-laying barge."

"You haven't worked off-shore in fifteen years. Where can you wear them now?"

"To the Bywater costume party tomorrow night. The theme is the newspapers and we're supposed to dress as our favorite headline."

"Ooh, fun! My favorite is those triplets born to the surrogate grandmother."

"Karen has come up with a theme for us. But it probably isn't that one."

"Karen?" Robin held the coffee pot tightly with both hands. "I saw your invitation to that party. I naturally thought you would be taking *me*."

Queens love Halloween, Carnival, and any other excuse to dress in outlandish costumes which would be illegal at any other time.

"Sorry, kitten. I've already promised Karen."

"I had a costume ready and everything."

"You can wear it on Mardi Gras."

"Vanna White might be passé by then."

He examined his reflection in the top of the sterling sugar bowl. "It's me less and less these days and Karen more and more. You're spending all your time with that fish."

"She was very depressed after what happened with Lucas."

"Yeah, I know. She thought he loved her and it was only her old man's money. I should have such problems."

"So as a good friend, I've been cheering her up."

"After almost four months, she should be cheered up the ass."

I let the subject drop, being too kind to tell him that I simply enjoyed conversation with one of my own people. One with wit, energy, and an I.Q. above sandwich level.

But my "significant other" wouldn't simply allow me to enjoy my coffee in peace.

"Matty?.. Matty, please look at me."

I didn't mind that part. The boy was still as cute as the day

I'd met him, with big brown eyes and golden hair. A ringer for Sandra Dee as "Gidget".

He took a deep breath. "You know we've been together three years now."

"Three years of rapture.—Turn the sound up."

He reached behind him and pressed the volume button distractedly. "And in all that time you've never made any real sign of committment."

The screen flashed "Mayor's Election" so I shushed him to hear the report.

"Latest polls show Armand Voitier pulling even further ahead at 31%. The liberal Moses Jones is somewhat behind, favored by 22% of those responding. The only Republican in the race, conservative Farley Berber, remains way behind at 18%."

That was encouraging.

The newscaster's voice deepened. "In what may be a related story, the murder of the well-known political consultant, Rodger Lloyd, remains unsolved. There is still speculation that Lloyd had died with his head on a book of bird illustrations in an attempt to name his murderer. All that is known is that Lloyd had contacted Sylvia Sinclair, a member of the prominent family."

Damn!

Robin resumed his blathering. "A committment! Did you hear?"

The commercial came on, so I gave him back my attention.

"What do you want, Robin? You don't have to work. I provide you with food, shelter, spending money, credit cards.."

"Sure, *now.* But all this is temporary. He waved at the window behind me. "What guarentee do I have that you won't throw me out the second I lose my looks?"

That particular window overlooked our back yard with its patio and crepe myrtle trees.

I didn't question his apprehension of being thrown into the back yard but just said, "You're only twenty-one."

"So? How much longer will I be twenty-one?„

"Ah.. Five months,.. fourteen days…"

"And then I'll be twenty-two. And after that twenty-three, with nothing to show for it!"

I put on my reasonable voice. "I'm sorry, kitten, but I can't halt the march of time. What do you want me to do about it?"

"Marry me."

"What?!"

I waited for a giggle or some other assurance that the suggestion was a joke but his face remained in its customary pout.

"Prove you mean it when you say you love me."

I had come to the table wanting only coffee, but now a shot of Bourbon would be in order.

"For pity's sake, Robin. I can see you dressing up like a girl and taking out a marriage license. But it still wouldn't be legal anywhere."

"I didn't mean the conventional way." He turned and rifled through a stack of papers on the buffet. "We can go to the Metropolitan Community Church and make a covenant of partnership just like David and Jonathan in the Bible."

"There's no Biblical basis for formalizing gay domestic arrangements."

He picked up a piece of gay literature printed on pink wood pulp and read, "Samuel: Chapter 18, Verse 3. Look it up."

"I'm familiar with the passage. But these gay marriage ceremonies are just a farce."

"We know other couples who've done it."

"Other couples have all kinds of ways of showing bad taste. There isn't a chance in the world that I would make myself such a public spectacle."

"It doesn't have to be public. We would just hold a reception for a few of our friends." He clasped his hands together like a road company Little Eva. "Simple handwritten invitations…"

"Register your silver pattern at Maison Blanche?"

"If they want to bring gifts.."

"And how about a swan carved of ice and some fat Italian singing 'Oh Promise Me'."

"Ooh, Matty, that would be glorious!" Then he halted mid-pirouette and hung the lip. "But you're being sarcastic, aren't you?"

"Very."

"I guess you think I'm expendable."

"Of course I don't, Kitten."

Of course he was. Who isn't?

CHAPTER FOUR
Tuesday Morning

At NOPD Headquarters on Broad Street, I negotiated the third-floor rabbit warren of partitions to Lieutenant Frank Washington's office. He saw me through the open door and waved me in.

"Grab a seat, Matt." He was evidently in the middle of brunch as a bag of beignets from the Café du Monde lay open on his desk. He brushed powdered sugar from his mustache. "Twelve years in the furniture business and now you're back into criminal law."

I pulled up a wooden chair. 'My law practice is like sex. I only do it for a few friends. How is the Lloyd investigation going?"

"It goes. M.E. confirms the victim died around noon on Saturday. We got that from the stomach contents." He flipped through a pile of forms for the typed narrative. "He ate breakfast at La Marquise. Viennese pastry."

"That's no way to start the day."

"It went down hill from there. He was stabbed in the back once. But when it's done right, once is enough. The body wasn't discovered till the maid came in to clean on Sunday."

"Hair and fiber samples?"

"Nothing. This isn't like a rape where the perp is all over his victim. The murderer never had to touch Lloyd."

"That's one for our side. A woman almost certainly would have left some hair around."

"Unless maybe it was plaited." He held up the report and placed it in front of me. 'Your cousin's wife hasn't been charged with anything yet. But she had a motive, an opportunity, no alibi, and well there's the 'dying message' pointing to Sylvia."

"There isn't enough to take to the D.A."

"On television they convict with less."

'In the newspapers too, unfortunately." I looked only at the bottom line of the report. "By person or persons unknown."

"I know Sinclairs hate publicity."

"Abominate it. But I've been mulling the case over, Frank. Couldn't Rodger Lloyd's 'dying message' have meant something else?"

"Like what?"

"Maybe 'warbler' referred to a singer."

"I considered all the possibilities.—Like a doughnut? No?— Female singers are called "thrushes" or "canaries" not 'warblers." Frank put a hand up to massage his scalp, maybe in the hope of reviving moribund hair follicles. "Then I wired the Chicago Police to look for someone named "borin" or something like it among the victim's acquaintances. I also looked for anyone who ever worked with feathers: arrow smiths, taxidermists, fan dancers.."

"I can see you're trying."

'Hey, I even went from the cuckoo angle and checked for anyone with a history of insanity. Guess what? That led us right back to Mrs. Sinclair."

"Insanity?"

"The lady was treated for severe depression on three occasions that we know about."

"Everone gets depressed."

"She had attempted suicide and had to undergo electro-shock therapy up in Pineville."

"I knew about her stay in the mental hospital."

"Which some irreverentlly refer to as 'the cuckoo's nest'." He turned his swivel chair toward the window to delight in his scenic view of Orleans Parish Prison. "A mentally unstable woman may do something crazy like.." He shrugged. "Kill a faithless lover who is threatening the sanctity of her home. All the clues point to Sylvia Sinclair."

"But it wasn't she."

"Just for fun, who's a more likely suspect?"

"There must have been people who had a better reason to do him in."

"So far as we know, the deceased was a stranger in town. Who could have worked up that much hate in three days? An undertipped bell boy?"

"The man must have been in touch with someone here. Let's assume first that Lloyd didn't come to New Orleans solely to meet Sylvia."

"You want me to assume that?"

"And assume that he didn't come for the crawfish either."

"Or the riverboat rides or the naked ladies on Bourbon Street? O.K.," He turned his palms out and spread his fingers in a lay benediction. "As a personal favor to you, I'll assume all those things."

"Lloyd must have come on business. The mayor's race is getting frantic right now. Suppose he was here to work with one of the candidates."

Frank clasped his hands behind his head. "Here I am, all worn out from assuming and now you want me to start supposing." He smiled tiredly. "Prove it Matt."

CHAPTER FIVE

Tuesday Evening

The Audubon Park stables are reachable via a circuitous route through the zoo grounds, over the railroad tracks, along the lake shore, then through the park. A small wooden sign, nearly obliterated by years and weather, is all that indicates its location. The only way to find the stables is to follow someone who has already been there.

When I pulled into the shell driveway, Pip was perched on the wooden rail of the paddock, slapping a crop against his boot. He called out to his riding student, an obese woman of middle-age who huffed and puffed around the ring astride a lazy Morgan.

"Watch your diagonal, Mrs Boudreaux! .. Heels down. Stretch those calf muscles."

I didn't call to him but stopped by the stable door to watch the lesson in progress. The owner, Karen Peloquin hailed me from inside the barn. "Hi, Matty! You almost didn't get to go out today. It rained pretty hard this morning."

Karen had gone through the usual adolescent girls' enamour of horses. But unlike most she never outgrew the obsession, so her dad bought her the stables as a college graduation present.

She lived in the house on the grounds and most of her life was centered around her horses. There can be worse lives.

She brushed dust and hay off her jodphurs, and threw her arms around me. "One more inch and you'd have to ride gators instead of horses."

"Yes, I hear those scaly green ones are good mudders."

"You're late, Matty."

"How did you notice?"

She kissed my neck. "I've missed you."

Her figure was generous and her copper-colored hair natur-ally curly. I was certain of that because it curled exactly the same way when we were three-year old "Don't Bees" together back in Miss Linda's Romper Room.

"I thought one Sinclair would hold you for awhile."

"That kid is your blood all right." She kept one arm around me as she turned to watch the lesson. "Philip is the youngest instructor we have, and also the best. His time is booked solid."

My nephew's voice carried across the ring.

"Shoulders back! Don't lean into your turns, Mrs. Boud-reaux. You're not riding a bicycle."

I shrugged as though only moderately consumed with pride.

"The boy knows his horses."

"Better than that, he knows his pupils. I think most of them are in love with him."

"Toes in, Edna! Once more around the ring at a trot. And if you manage to keep your back straight this time, I'll give you a kiss."

The plump back straightened perceptibly.

"Those women sure wouldn't accept any substitutes. I'm glad he's so reliable."

"He doesn't miss any lessons?"

"Never. Philip is here on the dot of nine every Saturday morning. I just wish I could get him more afternoons a week."

"School nights, he has to ride his algebra book."

In that moment, Mrs. Boudreaux's mount stopped to deposit a pile of manure in the middle of the track. An act more graceful than anything Mrs. Boudreaux was doing.

Karen stooped to accept a well-chewed stick from a particu-larly ugly mongrel dog. "At least some of the credit is yours, Matt. You pay for his lessons and drive him all over to the horse shows."

"I probably get more out of those competitions than he does. I'm reliving my youth."

"And then you went all out and bought Dickens for him."

She threw the stick into a clump of trees and the mutt tore off after it.

"That was his birthright, dear. Sinclairs and horses have always belonged together."

Having produced no sons of my own, I naturally expected George's to follow the family tradition. At least I could participate by financing their training.

On Ronald's fourth birthday, we brought him for his first riding lesson, as per Sinclair custom. But he was terrified at the very sight of the animal and shrieked so loudly that we never had the heart to put him through it again.

There was no such scene with Philip, a year later. From the beginning, he loved his riding sessions more than toys or television. He followed instruction precisely, took his spills without fear or tears, and by the time he was eight, looked like part of the horse.

"Your nephew has won every equitation trophy on the Southern Circuit. That's amazing for a male."

I took pretend umbrage. "For a male?"

She smiled coyly and looked a challenge at me. "Let's face it, Matt. Riding isn't a sport for men."

"We have the superior upper body strength."

"That's a handicap. You don't control a horse by brute strength; it takes technique and sensitivity." Karen ran her technically sensitive hands over my upper torso. "See, these heavy arm and chest muscles feel nice but they throw you off balance." She patted her own ample derrier. "Now a woman's lower center of gravity keeps her in the saddle. We're the natural equestrians."

"Then why are all the great jockeys male?"

"Politics."

"Ah."

"He'll be finished with Mrs. Boudreaux in a few minutes. Let's go inside."

Karen beckoned me to follow her through the stable door, under the horse shoe.

I said, "Speaking of politics, dear, how is the Uptown fund-raiser going?"

"Like a clock, Matty. The whole Garden District is coming out for Voitier. I'm going to meet with the group Thursday to collect on pledges."

"Your work could mean a difference of twenty thousand votes. Armand is very grateful."

"I'm glad to support him. He's the thinking man's candidate."

"We'll see how our man is coming over at the Bywater party tomorrow night."

Karen was coming off a bad love affair and I had two ways to relieve her misery. Involving her in my cousin's campaign was the second way. But she had taken up the cause so passionately that she was now considered the most important single element in the campaign.

"Who do you like today, Matty? Tam hasn't had a real work-out for a few days."

'She'll be glad to see me then. We'll go for a good gallop in the park."

Tam is a thoroughbred jumper belonging to my friend Edwina Devon Oakes. I don't keep a horse of my own any-more but several others let me ride theirs when they haven't the time. The horses need the exercise and so do my thigh muscles.

Karen slipped a halter over the mare's head and led her out of her box stall. "Want to curry her yourself?" She attached Tam's halter to the cross ties and handed me the hard comb.

"Right. The better to assess her mood." I held the mare by the halter and brushed in circular motions along her neck and shoulders. Grey dust came up in a light coating. "You must have been rolling in your stall, Tam."

Pip's horse Dickens was already being groomed by a stable hand called Chico. The gelding snorted in anticipation and tossed his head as much as the cross ties allowed.

On my first encounter with Dickens at the Texas Horse Auc-tion, I'd assumed he was named after the author of David Copperfield. But after one turn around the paddock, I came to guess a diabolical connotation as in "Ornery as the Dickens." This gelding would launch a war of the wills on every unsuspecting fool who tried to mount him, specializing in the one-two: full canter-dead stop maneuver. I don't like to begin every ride with a tug of war for control of my mount's head, but Pip always enjoyed the contest. He took the gelding for a few test rides and then would have that and no other for his thirteenth birthday.

I lifted the saddle and pad from the peg that said, "Tam" and adjusted them on her back, Karen stood by with the bridle. "Don't let Pip con you into racing and take a spill. I want you in good shape for tomorrow."

"Tomorrow?"

"I've been looking forward to it." She moved in and put her arms around me, her natural curls brushing my chin. "Last week you promised we'd spend all Wednesday together. Don't you remember?"

"Of course." (I hadn't.) "Very well, I'll stop by here around ten and we can go for breakfast at Brennan's."

"Umm. Ten is fine, but..." The curls tickled. "I think we ought to *do it* first and then go to breakfast."

"Fair enough. And then we'll—"

"Then we'll come back here and *do it*."

"Well,.."

"And then we'll take a ride up by the lake."

"That sounds good, but.."

"And then we'll come back here and *do it*."

"Karen, I don't think.."

"And then we'll take a walk along the levy. Of course that will make us feel really romantic so we'll want to.."

"Do it?"

"Yes!"

"Darling, when I was seventeen, I probably could have carried out such a program exactly as you describe it. But I had a much less strenuous schedule in mind for tomorrow. I was going to check out the three mayoralty candidates."

"I bet I know what you're thinking of!" Karen took her curls back. "Investigating Rodger Lloyd's murder?"

"Just asking a few questions."

"Oh, fun!" She leapt. "You're going to hunt down the real killer to protect Philip's mom!"

"I don't flatter myself."

"Let me come with you. I'll help."

"Sorry, but that's something I have to do alone."

"Very well." She threw her arms around my neck and jumped up to nuzzle me, her soft breasts rubbing my shirt-front on the way.

"If you prefer, we'll just lie around here and.."

"No! —I mean I can't!" I gave up and kissed her nose. "All right, dear. You can help me play detective."

"Great!" She wrapped me up in a hug just as Pip strode in, swinging his crop.

"Say, you two. The breeding paddock is around the other side."

Karen disengaged. "Your nephew has the Sinclair sexuality without its subtlety."

"Excuse the boy, please. At his age, he's too impatient to flirt."

She sighed, "The times we live in," and left us.

CHAPTER SIX

Tuesday Evening

Pip urged his mount into a fast trot through the parking lot.

"Do you want to race to the lake, Uncle?"

"Tam likes to warm up first, if you don't mind."

"I'll wait for you in the grove." Then he reined around, asked Dickens for a canter, and bolted ahead.

Tam and I started out at a brisk pace and caught up to him ten minutes later where he had halted under a live oak.

His blue eyes mocked. "We went around the park twice at a sitting trot and still had time for a short nap. Who do you think is getting old, Uncle? You or that mare?"

"Maybe we've just been inflicted with maturity and common sense."

"We'll ride together for awhile. Dickens and I will go easy on you." He was thoughtful a few moments before saying, "Karen talks about you a lot."

"We've been talking about each other for years·"

"I got the idea that it's serious lately. Marriage on your mind?"

"You know that's not likely."

"They say you came close to marrying Edwina Devon last year."

"I came close to considering it. Every man is prey to dynastic ambitions."

"You would marry just to have children?"

"Maybe, but I don't need them, thanks to you. You're everything to me that a son could be."

"Thank you." Philip beamed. "Then it's just casual between you and Karen."

"Casual fun and nice. Yes."

"Is she difficult to bring to orgasm?"

"Good grief!" I almost fell off the horse. "You're much too young to be discussing such things."

He lifted his shoulders. "That's what my parents think. Do you know I had to learn about procreation from Ronald? He was eight at the time."

"Where did Ronald learn?"

"From a book, of course. He'll probably never get any practical experience."

"Don't blame your parents. Most adults are shy about discussing sexuality with their kids."

"Especially their own sexuality. When I asked Mom and Dad where I came from, they claimed I was ordered from Holmes."

"Probably because Holmes has an unlimited return policy."

"Last year I found out that I was conceived during a thirty day leave when Dad was on his second tour in Viet Nam."

"George was a marksman in the Infantry. He used to come home on furlough in his uniform, covered with ribbons. Very impressive."

"Say, uncle, how did you manage to avoid the draft?"

"Uncle Sam didn't want me."

"Oh, I get it." He smiled roguishly. "They weren't taking fairies."

I laughed because I'm generally impervious to such digs. Especially from someone I love.

"Don't kid yourself. They took plenty of fairies. But no epileptics."

"Those fits of yours? My father told me how that happened. You cracked your head once riding."

"Correction. I never got hurt while riding. It was an abrupt stop that caused the damage. —I hit my head on a rail and after that the seizures started."

Dickens decided to canter without a cue and Pip had to rein him back to stay within chatting distance.

"I remember once when I was little, I saw you fall down and

start thrashing around and foaming at the mouth. I got scared, but then Mom said it wasn't serious and you felt nothing."

"I feel nothing during a grand mal seizure. Get a bitch of a headache afterward though."

He turned in the saddle to study me.

"You sound like it's no big thing. But I heard somewhere that epilepsy can be fatal."

"Almost never." Tam shook her mane as a horsefly lighted on her neck and I slapped it for her. "Usually the attacks last only a few minutes and no harm is done. But if I ever had a series of convulsions, one after the other, I'd probably die of asphixiation."

"How?"

"The breathing muscles would be in spasm."

"That's very frightening, uncle."

"No it isn't. Because so long as I take my pills I don't have seizures at all."

"Keep up with them then." Pip's mood lightened and he nudged Dickens into a fast trot. "Eyes ahead!" He pointed his crop up the trail toward an equestrienne astride a particularly fine Saddlebred mare.

"Isn't she gorgeous?"

"She should be. They tell me she cost $15,000 at the Southern American Saddlebred Auction."

Pip threw his head back and laughed. "I'm talking about the filly on *top*, uncle! Look at that terrific croup. She's got perfect confirmation. And I'd just like to climb aboard and hand-ride her all night."

"I know that lady, and believe me you'd be overmounted."

I spoke in an attitude of censure but my secret sentiment was, "Thank God he's not gay. They'd be blaming *me*."

We cantered past Geraldine, the only western saddle rider at the park, on her sway-backed Quarterhorse. The two of them poked along, looking as though they'd just come off a thousand mile cattle drive.

She deserved only a passing glance from my over-sexed nephew but at least that. No woman of child-bearing years escaped his notice. "Riding is the best sport there is for meeting girls. Almost everyone you see up are females. And the few guys in competition are like you."

"Handsome?"

"Gay. So I've got myself a clear field."

We cantered back to the stable yard, slowed to a trot in the driveway and dismounted. "Chico!'" I called into the barn. "Aqui esta Tam."

The groom appeared and took her bridle.

"Would you rather hose her off yourself, Señor?"

"No thank you. When you've washed one horse, you've washed them all."

"Some of the owners want to do everything themselves."

"Lady owners, right?"

"Well,.. Now that you say.. Yes, ladies."

"They think horses are babies with hooves and manes."

I know of women who spend three or four hours every afternoon at the stables fondly washing and brushing their mounts, feeding them carrots and cooing over them. They treat their horses like lap dogs, or even children, taking special pleasure in all these unnecessary attentions. I've always related to the horse as a dignified working animal, not a pet. And I'm sure they prefer it that way too.

CHAPTER SEVEN

Tuesday Night

He had to stop on the corner of Napoleon for a red light and a swarm of project children came running off the neutral ground with their squeegees to deposit some dirty water on my windshield and smear it around. I reached across Pip and deposited a quarter in the grubby little hand thrust through the window. They'd caught us fair and square.

Pip rubbed his palm over the shift in circles. 'Which way do you want to go, Uncle?"

"You're the driver. You choose."

"Then let's drive down St. Charles." He took the next left at Jefferson. "My favorite street."

"Everyone's favorite."

The most picturesque avenue in this postcard city of ours, St. Charles features giant oak trees, green street cars clanging down the neutral ground and, best of all, the stately old mansions. At least it's not immediately evident that most of those noble homes have (horribly) been transmogrified into condos or apartment buildings. But not ours.

Pip stopped on 1900 block, and executed a precise parallel parking. He turned the engine off to gaze at the finest home on the block, twenty-one rooms in three stories crowned by a red Spanish tile roof.

"The Sinclair House. I never get tired of looking at it." He pushed the power button to lower the back windows. "It's all yours, isn't it Uncle?"

"In title only, Pip. Remember that my mother has usufruct."

"Use a what?"

"Under Louisiana's 'forced heir' provision, Father had to leave me the house in his will. But he gave mother the usufruct, which is exclusive use of the property during her lifetime. She can do anything she likes with it but sell it.

He turned round in his seat. "And what she likes now is to rent it out to those nuns. What a drag."

"The Sisters of St. Martin use it for a nursing home. I don't mind. They're taking good care of the old place."

"But wouldn't you rather live here yourself?"

"Dear me, no! I couldn't afford to staff a house that size and keep it up. And Robin and I would just rattle around in all those rooms. I'm better off on Esplanade."

I saw a meter maid bearing down, so I signaled Pip to pull away from the curb before she had chance to block our way out and get my license number.

Pip stopped at the red light, still keeping sight of the house through the rear view mirror.

"That will be mine someday, won't it?"

"Yours and Ronald's, as my principal heirs."

"Forget Ronald. All he wants is space for his computer. My brother wouldn't know what to do with a place like that."

"And you would?"

He smiled and his teeth were perfect as befit his heritage.

"I'd go to my uncle Matt for advice on decorating."

The house on Banks Street had the faint smell of the illegal plant in the kitchen window box. I hoped Sylvia had burnt it to destroy it. She met us at the door clad in an Indian cotton blouse and flowered bell-bottomed hip-huggers. I'm old enough to remember when they fit her and she looked good in them.

"Thank you for picking up Philip, Matt." She reached out and stroked the boy's wheat colored hair. "I get scared when he comes home in the dark."

"But I'm going back out in the dark, Mom." Pip gave her a quick kiss. "Dance at school, remember?"

"Oh dear. When will you be back home?"

"Depends on my luck. —I mean the party might run late."

"You go out with girls three or four nights a week. I don't understand it."

She really didn't.

Ronald's door was open. He was guaranteed dull company but I had to pay my respects anyway. I stepped into his room where as always he was bent over the computer terminal.

"Hi Ronald."

"Hello, uncle Matt." He didn't look up.

"Are you going to the dance with Pip?"

"No, he has a date. I don't."

"You never will either if you don't pick up the phone."

"All that would get me are polite rejections. I think girls are attracted to guys who can ride." He moved the curser back and forth aimlessly. "Like my brother."

"If that's the issue, I'll spring for lessons anytime you like."

Ronald's glasses had slid down his nose and he pushed them back up.

"No thank you, uncle. I don't want to get on anything I can't control." He turned his attention back to the keyboard where he was evidently working on a program in CBasic. "Here, I am master of all I survey."

When I bought the gelding for Pip, I wanted to give Ronald something of equal value and he chose the computer and peripherals. Like no other Sinclair I've ever known.

"But you're also quite an athlete in your own right." I said with forced heartiness.

"Hmm. Got my third degree black belt last month," he mumbled as though it were no particular distinction.

Because he's small for his age, Ronald's father insisted that he learn judo as a means of self-protection. And the word was that he had excelled at the sport.

"Congratulations."

"Yeah."

I don't see how a sweaty, grappling conquest of an opponent your own size can compare with mastery over a spirited twelve hundred pound beast, for accomplishment or visual appeal. But in the interest of fairness, I would have been willing to go to Ronald's Judo matches and root for him as I did for Pip in horse shows. Fortunately, he never bothered to invite me, or even his parents. He would just enter his contests and tote home the trophies which looked rather puny next to his brother's grand brass equestrian figures.

I was racking my brain for another encouraging sentiment when Sylvia appeared in the doorway. I'd never thought I would so welcome her society. I even smiled.

"Matt?" Her voice was small and whiney. "George wants to rap with you about this bag I'm in."

So I followed her in to the usual conference place, the kitchen table, and she made a point of closing the door behind us.

Sylvia must have been expecting me this time, as her women's magazines had been tidily removed to the counter.

My cousin George was six feet two, fair, and well-favored like any Sinclair, but an unprepossessing figure now, slumping tiredly over a can of Dixie. Evidently not his first of the day. When I took the chair opposite, he looked up at me morosely. His eyes red.

"The cops are all assholes, Matt. My wife doesn't even have the strength to stab a man." He made two fists. "If she wanted to kill the creep she would have brought a pistol to do it. Even *Sylvia* has that much sense."

"They'll say she didn't have time to buy one."

"Didn't need to buy one. I've got a Taurus model thirty-eight Target Master in my bed table. Kept cleaned and loaded with fresh ammo at all times."

"The police believe she has a motive."

"I know all about that thing she had with Lloyd." He thrust out his chin. "Sylvia was naive in those days."

"Was she?"

"And that creep was some hot-shot college professor. Tall blond stud.."

"He reminded me of you, George," she offered dully.

"Yeah, sure. Anyhow, she was lonely. What happened happened."

Sylvia played with her braid. "I wasn't completely straight

with you before, Matt. My husband says I should tell it like it is."

"The truth? Fantastic." I turned a chair around and straddled it. "This will be a real treat."

She looked down at the stained formica. "Rodger ran out on me because...I told him I was knocked up."

"Pregnant?" My voice cracked like a teenager's.

"Really freaked me. I was so blissed out that I was about to bring this beautiful creature into the world."

For just the blink of an eye, Sylvia flashed some of the prettiness she must have had that day when she was young and glowing with the promise of life. In a time when other girls wore Indian cotton blouses and long braids. "I thought Rodger would be blissed out too."

"He wasn't blissed out?"

"Not at all. He told me it was my problem. He wasn't going to make a long term committment to some squirrel who was too stupid to take her pills." She stole a glance at her husband, but he wouldn't look up from his beer. "Rodger would have paid for me to go to Doc Knight. But an abortion would have been a denial of life, you know? Bad Karma."

"So Lloyd went back up north and you bore his child."

"My child."

"Did you tell your husband?" I asked as though he weren't there. Then all of a sudden he was.

"Who the hell cares!" He pounded the can of beer and it foamed. "When I visited her in Pineville, Sylvia told me she'd had that thing with Lloyd while I was in Nam and he'd got her pregnant. Period."

"George told me we should just forget it," she allowed humbly.

"And why the hell not?" The beer can spoke again. "Forget the war. Forget everthing that happened to us because of it. It's over."

I said, "Apparently Rodger Lloyd served to resurrect old memories."

Sylvia looked at her husband for permission to speak, but he was back to communing with his beer can. She went on with-out him.

"Rodger told me he had been married and divorced twice."

"So said the gossip columns."

She nodded. "But he bitched because both wives had given him only daughters. Four girls altogether. A son is what he wanted, so Rodger said he'd come back for his. What do you think of that?" A sidelong glance at her husband who hadn't moved. "He called my kid 'his' after all these years without a word."

"Lloyd wanted to establish a relationship with the boy?"

"I said 'No way, José!'. George is the boy's father now. But then Rodger lost his cool. He hollered that he had much more to offer because he was going to win this mayor's election for his client and get into a real success trip. He went on a lot about how he couldn't lose but I didn't care." She bit her lip. "Then he said he had a right. That's not true, is it?"

"Only what you give him."

"Zip then. That's what I figured. So then Rodger flipped out and threatened to introduce himself to our son so he could decide for himself."

"So that was the reason for the letter. To beg him not to."

"To leave the boy alone. For his own sake." She stirred her coffee with a pencil.

George drank the beer down. "Anyhow the kid has never known any father but me and I want to keep it that way."

"How much do you want to keep it that way?"

"Not enough to kill Rodger Lloyd if that's what you mean. But anyhow I never even knew the creep was in town."

"I couldn't bring him into it," Sylvia said. "You know how George goes out of his tree."

There wasn't a word among us for the next two minutes.

When at last I broke the silence, my throat was dry.

"Which of the boys was Lloyd's? Pip or Ronald?"

Sylvia stiffened and met my eyes defiantly. "I never told any-one. Not even my husband."

"It doesn't matter!" George thumped the table with both

fists. "They're both mine now!"

Sylvia flinched at the gesture then clutched his arm. "It matters to him though. Don't you get it? He's afraid of leaving his money to a fake Sinclair. Isn't that it, Matty?"

I didn't answer her because that was it.

"Fuck him then!" George jumped up so fast that he knocked his chair over backwards and I too sprang to my feet in an adrenalin rush for fight or flight. "Well, we never asked for your goddamned money. Not my wife and me and not the boys either!"

Sylvia cringed, then leaned over and righted the chair.

"Please George. Matt's good people."

George upped to me then. His eyes were angry and I felt his hot breath on my face. "Who the hell needs you? I teach my kids real values. To work with their *hands*!" He held up a large and calloused one. "I teach them how to set a volt-ohm meter, wire a circuit, so they'll grow up to be useful! All you do is prance around here like a big shot and put fancy ideas in the kids' heads! You got them acting like rich men's sons."

I backed away from him. "I'm sorry George. I didn't think I was giving them anything they shouldn't have."

He flung open the refrigerator door and grabbed another beer. "Just because you're not man enough to make kids yourself, you got to come in here and try to steal mine!"

"I didn't mean to—"

He slammed the refrigerator door and a dozen little magnets shaped like "Peanuts" characters fell and bounced on the grungy linoleum. "We don't need your goddamn interference in our lives! My wife never killed anyone and the police can't touch us!"

On that note he stomped out of the kitchen to leave Sylvia and me basking in the awkwardness of the moment.

She sighed heavily and busied herself picking up the magnets. "I'm sorry, Matt. He should try to go with the flow, but he just, like, freaked."

"I know he did."

"He'll cool down. Of course he's grateful for everything

you've done for the boys. George is only bummed out because he was never able to give them those, like, material things himself." She finger-polished that little black haired girl who always pulls the football away from Charlie Brown. "He just can't get into this poor relation bag. I'm afraid he's a very young soul."

"No, I'm the one at fault. I picked up a Linus that had landed under the table. "George is right that I've always wanted sons of my own. So I guess I've been usurping his." That was too much to admit and I felt my throat tighten. "I'll continue to pay all the bills that come to my office. But I won't try to see the boys again."

She rubbed a Snoopy between her hands. "You can see them any time you want, Matt. George just expects you to pretend they're both his the way he does."

"That's why he got so angry."

"The kids themselves haven't a clue, see? Nobody but me ever knew which isn't my husband's."

"Lloyd must have known which."

"How? I never told him."

"If you already had a child when you met, he knew his would be the younger son."

"Oh.." She looked vacant. "Yeah maybe that way. But I wouldn't give him the name."

"He could have read their names right off those trophies in the living room. And the name of their school too. It would have been easy then to hunt them down."

"But he didn't, right? He was croaked before he had a chance to do anything."

"So we must assume."

CHAPTER EIGHT

Wednesday Morning

I opened the car door for Karen and she crossed her legs provocatively before swinging them under the dash board to imbue me with an appreciation of the new short skirts.

"This detective business is going to be fun. Are we playing Nick and Nora today?"

I settled behind the wheel then had to reach across her to buckle her in. "You're too buxom to play Nora. Let's try Perry Mason and Della Street."

'I feel very 'Forties Era' today. I'm dressed for a sophisticated comedy in black and white." She smoothed the skirt of her oyster peplum suit. "It's great to get out of stable clothes for a change."

"You may wish you had worn them. We're going to be interviewing politicians."

She wrinkled her nose which looked cute even wrinkled and checked her make-up in the visor mirror.

"Fair enough, Perry. Where do we stand in the *Case of the Butchered Birdwatcher?*"

"For our basic premise, you and I know that Sylvia didn't kill Rodger Lloyd."

"Got it, chief—How do we know that?"

"Because Pip needs a mother."

"Oh!… Very well then. So what about her husband George? He could have been listening on the extension when Lloyd called his wife, and he must own a fishing knife, so.." Then she saw me glowering and caught herself. "Oops! Okay, George is out because Pip needs a father, Right?"

"Right. So who else knew Lloyd was in town? I'll answer my own question. The man who hired him to come down here. One of the candidates.

"If Armand had called him in, he would have told us."

"But suppose someone else had called him on Armand's behalf?"

"Is that possible?"

"Are the Saints having a winning season? Anything is possible."

"So today we're going to conduct an unofficial and underhanded investigation of him and the other two candidates. Moses Jones and Farley Berber."

"Our first stop will be Berber's western wear store out on Veteran's Highway."

"I used to see his commercials all the time. They're awfully cornball but he sells a lot of cowboy suits."

"Now he's trying to sell himself."

The front of "Berber's Rodeo Emporium" was enclosed by a fake aluminum "split-rail" fence. We walked through the swinging doors past a polyester "Indian blanket", a plastic sun-bleached Longhorn skull and a display of "portly jeans" at "Twenty percent below cost!"

Right.

A black "cow girl" with a "Ya'at" accent directed me to her boss's back office. The door was held wide open with a fake anvil so we didn't scruple to walk through it.

"Hello Farley. Do you have a minute?"

"Why if it ain't Matt Sinclair, sure as shootin'."

Berber stood up and shook my hand. "And who's that purty cowgal ye got there?"

"This is Karen Peloquin, my... assistant."

Karen looked concerned. "Cowgal?"

But she stepped forward to offer her hand politely. "You look just the same as on T.V.." She tried to make it sound like a compliment, which no reference to our host's appearance could honestly be.

Farley Berber was over six feet tall and lanky, a dry stalk of a man. And he exacerbated the problem by wearing cowboy boots and an electric blue western suit that made him look like a swizzle stick. His features would have been called "Lincolnesque" by the sympathetic. The less-so might resort to some expression like "would stop an eight-day clock". The unlovely visage was crowned by limp graying hair in a bowl cut with a cowlick. Here stood the epitomic yokel.

He issued us a warm country grin-too-big-for-his-face which he'd probably copied from Andy Griffith and indicated his Long Branch style bar. "Belly up and he'p yoreselves."

"Thank you but we've both just.. bellied."

"Then y'all pull up a coupla stumps and take the load off your feet." Fortunately real chairs were available and we took them and reconnoitered Berber's office.

The room had become a hybrid of ersatz frontier sheriff's office and campaign headquarters with "Berber For Mayor" posters tacked up over Frederic Remington prints, and stacks of election literature held down with prop peace pipes and tomahawks. A painstaking replica of a Sharp's Carbine 50 buffalo gun adorned the inside wall. The color and dimensions were exact and it would have passed for genuine if gunsmiths of the Civil War era had worked in plastic.

I picked up one of the campaign leaflets, printed in red, white, and blue. Moses Jones's picture was on the left, looking black as a minstral player in burnt cork. My cousin Armand Voitier was on the right in a photograph over-exposed to make him look as dark as possible. The place of honor at center was for Berber, of course. The great caucasion hope of urban politics. I tapped the picture.

"It appears that you're the only white man running this time."

"Don't make no never mind. Last two mayors we had was black. White don't do me much good."

I couldn't see another advantage in the world of displaying his picture except to show his whiteness.

"I'm real tickled about your visit here," he went on. "Voitier ready to give up and th'ow me his support?"

I chuckled along with him then got down to cases.

"We're looking into the murder of Rodger Lloyd."

"Poor critter got himself stabbed?" He betrayed no interest.

"We're trying to trace his last movements. Did you contact him to come in as your image consultant?"

"Heck, no. I got me an image already. You think I need to change it?"

"Like a baby needs milk," I thought. But what I said was, "Maybe you would try some last minute repositioning to salvage your campaign."

"My campaign is goin' jes fine, thank you."

"But you're running a distant third in the polls."

"Who cares?" He stretched his long legs out to his ottoman, a wooden "powder keg" which had probably never held anything but his feet. "Hardly figured I had a Chinaman's chance, goin' in. No other Republican around here wanted the job so I got up the five hundred dollar filing fee and had a go."

"I get it. You offered yourself as a candidate to get free publicity for your business."

"Yer dern tootin'. The Republicans pay for my posters and air time. They sent this fella, Ollie Dunn, to tell me where to go and what to say and ever' body sits up 'n' takes notice. Hey, that's a lot of attention for a poor country boy."

"You have no political ambition then."

"I'm already a man of means, doin' pretty well with my bidness here. What else do I need?"

The question was rhetorical but got answered anyway in the next moment when Berber's wife, Kim, slunk through the doorway in a cloud of Opium perfume. He caught his breath at the sight of her and rose out of his seat.

Petite and exotic, she had black, nearly waist-length hair and was as stunning as her husband was homely. There was nothing remotely country about Kim Nguyen Jefferson Berber in her Gianni Versace wool suit with mid-thigh length skirt, straight out of Vogue. This woman would have disdained even to set foot in such a place as "Berber's Rodeo Emporium" if she hadn't had access to the till.

Without a word to any of us she took a pack of Gauloises from her purse and liberated a cigarette.

Like most pretty women, Karen is fascinated by a beautiful one and couldn't take her eyes off the oriental femme fatale. But I was watching Farley and the way he seemed to diminish in Kim's presence, stooping more at the shoulders, aging and growing meeker as if she were sapping his strength and virility by her mere proximity.

I'd never seen a man that weak on his own wife. He brought the ignominious state of being "pussy whipped" to a new height and depth.

"Hi there, Matty," Kim said with a bare trace of accent. She ignored Karen and bent over me teasingly proferring her little gold lighter. I don't believe in lighting cigarettes for anyone but I did hers to avoid a scene. She executed a French inhale. "Long time."

"Quite. I haven't seen you since.. before you were happily married."

A frown flickered on and off to be replaced by a brittle smile. Kim was a survivor.

I'd first met this flower of the Orient in the mid-sixties shortly after she had come to the U.S. as the pregnant bride of a black G.I., Private First Class Clerow Jefferson of Gretna. It didn't take her long to get the lay of the land. Segregation was still the law as well as the fact in Louisiana and Kim soon realized that she was on the wrong side of it, economically speaking. So she left her husband and baby back in their West Bank project and moved across the river.

The girl had very little to work with in those days, afflicted as she was with acne, bad teeth, and a body with no womanliness in it. But never lacking industry or ambition, the skinny Viet Namese immigrant worked sixteen hour days as a bar maid and B drinker in the seamans' dives on Canal Street, turning tricks in the ladies' room at Lucky's and saving her money. When she'd acquired enough to finance dentistry, face-planing and silicone implants, she was able to improve her product and move across town.

Kim hit on a new marketing technique back during the Masters & Johnson rage, and built up a profitable business "counseling people with sex problems."

She "counseled" them every way but loose as I remember.

"We've been very happy for nearly two years. Isn't that right, dear?" Mrs. Berber flashed the three carat marquis cut diamond on her ring finger, focusing on that instead of her husband. And who could blame?

"Happy as a mule eatin' briars." He made as if to pat his wife's thin shoulder but she shifted slightly so that he flapped at air.

We had driven twenty blocks down Vet's Highway and hit the I-Ten ramp back to New Orleans when Karen broke into my thoughts.

"You haven't said anything since we left Berber's. What are you brooding about?"

'Mules don't eat briars.'"

"What's that?"

"They do not. You know I used to spend my summers on 'Nonc' Aldus's farm."

"Sure, way up there in Cajun country. So?"

"So, I know mules. Well, maybe if one were starving he would *try* to eat briars, but he most assuredly wouldn't be happy about it."

"Of course not. But I don't see how that—"

'Now a jack-ass would eat briars. A jack-ass would eat just about anything. He wouldn't be happy about it either. But those briars would stretch his mouth out so he would *look* like he was grinning, see?"

'Okay, but what does that have to do with—?'

'The old country expression goes 'grinning like a jack-ass eating briars' and Berber's got it all wrong."

"A natural mistake."

"Natural because he's a complete *phony*. The only mules that city slicker ever saw were pulling tourists around the Quarter in shiny red carriages. What's more, *nobody* is 'dern tootin'' these days. Do you know anyone who's 'dern tootin'?"

"No. I don't"

"Even Festus was never 'dern tootin'. If George 'Gabby' Hayes were still alive today, even *he* wouldn't be 'dern tootin'."

By now we had hit the overpass above the Superdome. The towering billboard advertised the Saints game for Sunday.

Karen pulled down the visor mirror and freshened her lipstick.

"So, Farley Berber's a phony. Aren't most politicians?"

"But in his case, I'm going to find out just how phony."

"You're right."

I had my answer fifteen minutes later at Armand Voitier's headquarters, a store front in Gentilly.

Armand had stood up to shake my hand. Distinguished in steel-rimmed glasses, he was tall like most Voitier-Sinclairs. (At only five-nine, I'm the runt of the clan.) And this particular afternoon he looked strange and bare in a short-sleeved shirt.

Armand Voitier's entire demeanor and personality called for a three piece suit which he wore in every photograph and to every function. I'd sort of assumed he slept in one.

My cousin was officially a quadroon if you want the arithmetic of it, so he had enough caucasion blood to pass the old Autocrat Club tests. His tawny complexion was lighter than the hue of a grocery bag and his hair had just a slight curl to allow a fine-toothed comb through it. His wife, Claudia, was fairer still and any Yankee would take her for white.

He had pushed aside a box of campaign flyers, given his chair to Karen and waved me to a seat on a cardboard crate.

"We researched both opponents down to their ankles, Matt. If you want the data on Berber... Eddie, give it to him."

Armand's law partner, Ed Stokes, was a small and dapper man who wouldn't give up his own suit even for rough work in hot weather. He picked up a type-written sheet and read tonelessly:

"Farley Berber grew up in Atlanta and graduated from the

University of North Carolina with a degree in Business Administration."

"So he isn't the unschooled bumpkin he would like to appear."

"Nothing rural about him. His father, Isaac Berber, had a clothing store on Peachtree Avenue. Started with one and finished with three. Farley started with the three and worked them up to a chain of twenty-seven 'Rodeo Emporiums' throughout the South-East."

"A real shrewdie."

Armand picked up a video tape cassette. "That country boy posture is good for business though. Would you like to see one of his commercials?"

"I don't think I would enjoy that much."

Too late. The tape was in and running.

Armand had made himself comfortable on the edge of the desk to indulge in a moment of light entertainment.

"Naturally, he hasn't run these since he announced. We got a bootleg copy."

I'd already seen T.V. ads for Berber's Rodeo Emporium. But in this context, I could understand why Armand was so encouraged by it, smiling and stroking his mustache.

The set was reminiscent of a children's show back in the early fifties: dressed to convey a bunk house. There was a wall of prop winchesters, a bale of hay, and, center stage, a saw horse holding a western saddle. Berber straddled this, clad in a shiny silver cowboy suit. He looked like a pair of tongs.

"Y'all come on out here to Berber's Ro-day-o Emporium!" he whooped to the television audience. "You'll find bargains the likes o' which you ain't seen since the ol' country store with a pot bellied stove. No sir. We got jeans in every size from slim on up to portly and boots of every hide. Whoo-whee! Vet's Highway in Kenner. It's an easy drive with free parkin' fer yore horse and rig…"

Karen looked embarrassed. "That clown aspires to be our next mayor?"

Armand shrugged. "Personally, I think the guy's a disgrace

to the Republican party, but what can we do? He's wrapped up the racist vote."

"Unless they find out he's a Jew." Ed Stokes offered slyly.

Armand crumpled a sheet of scrap paper. "We're not going to touch that." He aimed for the waste basket and sunk it. (Basketball star at Brother Martin.) "If we call him on being Jewish, he'll have to take the position that he was proud of it all along. Then he'll start speaking Yiddish and waving the flag of Israel. Then to prove I'm not anti-semitic I'll have to go around eating bagels and quoting from the Talmud." He shook his head. "There goes at least half my black support."

Ed smirked at me. "Blacks hate Jews."

"I know."

'On a much more pleasant note," Armand slapped his knee. "I'm glad you brought Karen to see us. I've been wanting to thank her personally for all she's done on the campaign."

She smiled. "Just invite me to the victory party."

"You're making it a victory party. Your canvassing uptown may be the difference between winning and losing."

"I hope so." Karen leaned forward. "I can't do enough for Matt's cousin."

"Half-third cousin." I said. "Our common great-great grandfather was Maximillian Sinclair."

"The biggest plantation owner in three parishes," Armand added. "His first wife, Matt's ancestor, was Acadian. After she died, he married my ancestor, Therese Voitier, a freed woman from the West Indies. Our line hyphenated the name to distinguish ourselves from the white branch of the family. Then eventually we dropped the Sinclair."

Karen looked from one to the other of us, assessing the resemblance. "That must have been around the War between the States."

"Maximillian was killed at Shiloh. Then his sons, and every other able-bodied Sinclair male fought for the Confederacy," I said. "Both white and colored."

Ed whistled. "You better not let that get out, Armand. That your ancestors were racists."

"I don't show my 'Sons Of The Confederacy' card around. That's for sure.—Please help yourself to some soft drinks. I'm sorry we don't have anything harder."

"Karen and I didn't come to drink. We're on an unofficial investigation."

She stood up. "*The Case of the Butchered Birdwatcher.*—I'm getting a diet something."

'You mean that murder in the Quarter? A Sinclair was mentioned in the papers." An unaccustomed frown. The Sinclair name published in any but a context of charity and public service was a blight on us all.

"Sylvia is married to my first cousin, George. Someone at the police station called the media before I even knew what happened. I couldn't keep her name out."

"The George Sinclairs? We don't hear much about that branch."

"They're .. private people. Until yesterday." Karen was looking over the selection of soft drinks. I held up a finger. "A diet cola for me, dear. Double the caffeine. I need it.—The man murdered was named Rodger Lloyd."

"I've heard of him," Armand said. "Eddie?" Ed Stokes was apparently the human data bank of the office. He already had the relevant paper in his hand "Rodger Lloyd has been plying his trade around the country nearly ten years. He worked for losing candidates in New York, Chicago, and Los Angeles. Winning ones in Youngstown, Albany, Portland, Omaha and Fargo. When we announced six months ago, he offered his services at his usual rates."

"Not interested." My cousin shook his head. "Imagine some yankee coming down here and telling me how to appeal to my own friends and neighbors. Ludicrous."

"For you, yes. But maybe the other candidates weren't so sure of themselves."

"Well, Matt. Poor Farley Berber needs all the image help he can get. A complete overhaul from the skeleton out."

"Agreed. But he denies contacting Lloyd."

"You're other choice is my worthy opponent to the left,

Moses Jones. But I think he's a little less likely to ask a white man for help than to slow dance with Al Campanis."

"I agree. But Karen and I are going to pay him a call anyway."

CHAPTER NINE
Wednesday Afternoon

Moses Jones had established headquarters on Canal Street, just two blocks from the Iberville Project. So his constituents were able to walk in anytime to discuss their political concerns, pick up leaflets for distribution, and incidentally to enjoy the free coffee and sandwiches donated by the good ladies of the First Zion Baptist Church. This was an especially popular gathering place near the end of the month when the food stamps ran out.

We stepped carefully through the store so as not to bump distracted mothers or tread on their crawling infants. Karen looked slightly anxious in this alien milieu and clung to me as I addressed the person in charge, an enormous woman of color who sat at a card table stuffing envelopes with a wide-eyed baby on her lap. She glanced up from her work and called behind her to the back office.

"Moses? White folks out here."

The baby, sucking at his bottle filled with pop, had no comment.

Jones was a slim and dramatically handsome man of a very dark complexion. His campaign issue was that he was the only true black man running. He hadn't even bothered to court white voters but spent all his media dollars in ads on black radio stations. His credentials as an early civil rights worker were mentioned in the ads. His degree from Harvard Law was not.

At the first sight of me, he assumed a chin-out debater's stance. But then he relaxed and smiled. "Hi Matt. For a second there I thought you were some kind of white reporter."

"Just some kind of white." I shook his hand and introduced Karen.

"Miss Peloquin, the campaign fireball of the Garden District. I wish I had you on my side."

"I'm flattered," she said graciously.

"Are you two here on a spy mission for Armand?"

"That of course. But also we're looking into the matter of Rodger Lloyd."

"The political consultant?"

"Did your people call him in?"

"Are you jazzing? Lloyd only worked for white candidates."

"He contacted Armand."

A self-righteous smile. "Exactly what I told you. Voitier is white everywhere except on his birth certificate. And don't think our people don't know it."

"Save the rhetoric. I'm trying to find out who murdered a man."

"Three or four poor blacks are murdered every single week in this city. And there's no fancy dressed investigator coming around."

"In ninety-five percent of those cases no investigation is necessary because they're domestic quarrels. Most of the rest are drug related."

"Correctly implemented social programs will cut into those statistics."

"Who's going to pay for them?"

He was sorting through his mental files for a pre-recorded answer when a scrawny boy about eight peered through the open door then crept in slowly as though afraid of being beaten for his timerity. Jones pivoted on a dime, deftly snatched the boy in both hands and swung him up to eye level.

"'Bout tahm you came see me, Eustis. Way you been keepin' yo lil' butt?"

"I be stayin' by my mama's Mr. Moses," was the plaintive reply. "Only she and Travis done went off someway, yestiddy."

"You gitchu ass ovah by the table an' take you one o'them

samitches. And drink you milk wit' it, not pop. Heah?"

"Yes suh, Mr. Moses." Eustis made his way to the refreshment table, still looking around as though he were about to steal. Jones winked at me.

"You see the advantage of knowing a second language?"

"I'd bet your sandwiches will be the boy's main meal of the day."

"You'd win." He sighed and lit a cigarette. "His mother turns her money and food stamps over to her pimp. She keeps Eustis with her just long enough to apply for welfare then hands him off to anyone willing to take him." He inhaled the smoke as though it were life-giving oxygen. "Multiply him by hundreds. Thousands."

What can you tell me about Lloyd?"

"I know nothing personally. And nothing has been coming up from the street either. So I'd bet my new stick pin it wasn't a simple mugging for love or money."

I held Karen's hand as we walked back up South Claiborne. Not out of any desire to act straight but simply because that's the natural way to walk with a woman.

When we had passed the grave yard with its ancient mausoleums of marble and granite still visible over the brick walls, she asked, "What do you think of Moses Jones?"

"At least he's not a phony."

"A Harvard man who speaks in urban black jargon?"

"Yes, but he's sincere about what he's doing." We crossed the street to the parking lot under the I-Ten overpass. "He could have exploited poor little Eustis by sticking him up on a campaign poster. He could have used any of them. But he didn't."

"You sound like you admire the man."

"Why not? Moses is educated, intelligent, honest and idealistic."

"Then we're only breaking our tails supporting Armand because he's your cousin?"

"Because he can do the best for the city. Remember that Armand has the savvy, the connections and the standing to upgrade our tourist industry, bring more conventions to the area, and promote tax incentives to keep profitable businesses from leaving. My cousin has been a politician all his life."

"And devoted to the interests of the main line oligarchy while Moses insists on being his own man."

"Hardly 'his own man', dear. Moses is getting his strings pulled by Nat Ortigue himself."

"The contractor?"

"And reigning patriarch of all the black labor unions in the city. He's got enough money to buy the Voitier-Sinclairs for breakfast. All self-made."

"But I've heard Nat Ortigue is very conservative."

"A little to the right of Vlad the Impaler."

We reached the car and once again I was relieved that it had survived parking in a public area without being vandalized. I unlocked Karen's door then went around to the driver's side. She reached across the seat to unlatch mine.

"So why would a capitalist like Ortigue be interested in the poor man's candidate, Moses Jones?"

"Ortigue has one of everything but a mayor. —Seat belt?— Naturally, he couldn't buy Armand. But Moses fell within his price range."

"Expensive hobby." She handed me the buckle and I fastened it for her.

"But lucrative. Once his man is in office, how many city construction projects will fall in his lap?"

"Don't they have to call for sealed bids on those, and take the lowest?"

"Theoretically. But suppose the council decides there's an 'emergency' repair job needed?"

"Like a crack in a levy?"

"Or a really big pot hole. No time for bids, right? Well, we'd better call in that old reliable, Ortigue Construction."

"So that's how they get around it."

"Even when the council does open bids they can find reasons not to take the lowest. This is New Orleans."

"Do you think Moses would 'knuckle under', to Ortigue

once he gets in office?"

"He probably thinks he won't. Give him that."

CHAPTER TEN

Wednesday Evening

I was grateful that my off-shore work clothes still fit me after fifteen years. Karen, for her part, was costumed in a "Bo Peep" style pinafore with matching sun bonnet. Thus attired, we parked on Alvar Street and walked up Burgundy to Pauline, guided by the lights and noises of the Halloween party.

Bywater is a "re-gentrifying" neighborhood in the notorious Ninth Ward. After forced integration in the sixties, the white middle class fled to the suburbs and the fine old homes of the Ninth were re-zoned and converted into multiple dwellings. A few years ago though, some baby boomers got bored with the brick cracker boxes in their monotonous tracts and came back to the city and Bywater. They bought the houses for triple what their parents had sold them for and reconverted to single homes.

Bywater now comprises equal parts white and black. But the white contingent remains invisible most of the time, only emerging from behind iron gates and burglar bars for neighborhood meetings or the occasional party. At least once a year, the movers and shakers of Bywater collectively put aside their zoning reports and renovation projects to dress up, get drunk, and carry on.

Tonight, security was provided by two policemen leaning against their blue and white out front. They glanced at our costumes and waved us down the alley way to the fete in the back yard.

The property was well-fenced and guests were greeted at the end of the alley by the chief hostess, Joanie. In keeping with the "Favorite Headlines" theme, she was dressed as the Pope.

"Hi, Matt!" She gave me a hug, swathing me in yards of white satin. "So glad to see you even if it's only once a year."

I handed her my invitation. "The event of the season. I wouldn't miss it."

Karen said, "I'm sorry. I misplaced my invitation."

Joanie laughed. "No problem. I know you, Karen."

"Not tonight." My date threw a salute off her bonnet. "Tonight I'm Baby Jessica. And Matty is one of those brave oil field workers who pulled me out of the eighteen inch pipe. "

"Congratulations. The band is great tonight. We'll have costume judging at eleven and mud-wrestling at twelve."

"I hadn't known there would be a major athletic contest."

"Carol and I have been sparring all week. Get a table ringside and bet on me." Our hostess pointed to the table behind her. "Before you wallow into the crowd though, you've got to vote for our next mayor."

Bywater's annual straw poll is our best barometer of the "Big Chill Generation" vote, and I always take an interest in the results.

Karen and I each took a paper ballot, scribbled "Voitier" and pushed it into the ballot box. Joanie boldly watched over our shoulders. "That's the way it's going tonight. Mostly Voitier." She turned away to greet four celebrants in grape masks who held out their invitations.

I took Karen's hand and channeled our way through the crowd pulsing to the rhythms of the five piece group. An ersatz Bork in judge's robe and stringy beard of twine spilled scotch on a jitterbugger who had decorated his balding head with red ink to represent Gorbachev. Interns and residents from Charity Hospital "disguised" themselves in surgical greens and wore signs touting "Beer Therapy". Some women had improvised a look by simply putting on two much eye make-up and letting it run to suggest Tammi Faye Bakker. Ollie North was the most popular figure of the evening, as several guests in fatigues hefted their bundles of shredded paper. We waded through Arab arms dealers, Iranians, and Contras. One wag portrayed

Gary Hart by the easy device of blow-drying his hair and leaving his trousers unzipped.

I found us a table near the mud-wrestling pit then made my way to the bar for our drinks. Ivan Boesky was on line ahead of me, hand-in-hand with Max Headroom.

I knew Jake, the head bartender, and he knew me.

"Sazerac for you, Matt," he said as a fact. "What else?"

"Pink Squirrel."

"Oh, are you with Robin tonight?"

"A *real* girl."

"Great! I knew you'd come around."

Back at the table, Karen was saving my seat with her feet.

"I'm glad we're not near the speakers. I've got to tell you something."

I served her drink and displaced her feet. "Listening."

"Wait a minute." She bent over her glass and took a long sip through the straw. "Good. Ooh, they're playing 'Through The Eyes Of Love'. Let's dance."

I gave my Sazerac a swallow of approval then took her in my arms. The patio was crowded with our fellow middle-aged romantics so we staked our claim of two square feet of lawn under stars and colored lights and danced close. I approved of her Diva.

She twirled a lock of my hair around her finger.

"I love your cologne."

"That's aftershave. Cologne is for sissies."

"Matty?" Abruptly, she stopped moving. "The something I've got to tell you.. Brace yourself because here it is: I'm pregnant."

"Opf?" I almost tripped over her left foot. "But how could you be..?" My heart threatened to crash through my rib cage. "We always use.."

"Not from you. I'm at least five months along." She looked at once guilty and frightened. "I wasn't being careful with Lucas because I thought I wanted his child. We *were* planning to get married."

We had stopped dead still in the middle of the rocking throng.

I held her tightly and resumed our claustrophobic waltz.

"How long have you known?"

"More than two months. My period was late so I bought one of those home pregnancy tests. I set the plastic jar up on my desk and went for a trail ride. That gave me one hour to think about Lucas." Karen put her arms around my neck and held on for dear life. "How he wanted me to sell the stables and invest in some scheme of his. I just couldn't marry him, could I?"

"Of course not."

"When I got back to my office, the tube showed this tell-tale ring. I didn't know whether to be happy or miserable."

I made some kind of soothing noise while thinking: Five months? That's too long. Too late.

"I considered .. you know.. not having it. But.." She buried her head in my chest. "Well, I'm thirty-nine, Matty. This may be the only chance I have to be a mother. I'd better let nature take its course."

"I understand."

"I'm so glad." She looked more relieved than glad. "I've ordered some literature about Lamaze classes. And now.. I'm going to need a coach."

"A coach?" My head was swimming.

"I know this is a lot to ask." Her nails were dug into my arms. "Would you please come with me and help me breathe?"

"I..?" At the moment I couldn't think of anything I'd enjoy less than seeing a woman go through labor with another man's child.

Agree now and try to get out of it later. That's all I could do. I held her against me.

"Of course, darling."

"Oh, thank you! I knew I could count on my dearest friend. Now I need that drink." She slid her arm down mine and caught my hand as we moved back to the table. "At least no one absconded with our drinks."

I pulled Karen's chair out for her and she leaned over to sip her Pink Squirrel. "Here's to the future."

I held up my Sazerac. "To the next generation. May it—
"Karen!! What's wrong?!"

Her eyes were bugged out in a horrific stare. And in the next second she had doubled over and thrown herself violently to the ground where she writhed in breathless agony.

CHAPTER ELEVEN
Wednesday Night

"We were able to save Miss Peloquin. But I'm sorry. She lost the child."

The doctor had put a hand on my shoulder and spoken with professional sympathy, assuming no doubt that I had sired the lost innocent.

My relief, though, was unmitigated. I might have felt some regret for the baby, but women of our circle do not bear and raise illegitimate children.

"May I see her?"

"I guess that would do her good. But only for a moment."

Karen seemed to be asleep till I was directly over the bed, then she opened her eyes halfway. She looked almost as pale as the sheet and very young without any make-up. Her voice too was weak and childlike.

"Hi, Matty. I'm sorry I ruined the mud wrestling match."

I pulled up a chair and took her hand.

"There's always next year."

"Thanks for saving my life."

"You kidding? There were three doctors at the party. They flew to your rescue and got that half & half down your throat. Then the cops rushed you over here to the stomach pump."

"But someone had to tell them my drink was poisoned." Some strength came into her hand. "Who would want to kill me? Who do you think?"

"Darling, I can't imagine."

"I don't have any enemies... Listen, Matty." She lowered her voice to a whisper. "I must have been poisoned because we're tracking down Rodger Lloyd's killer."

"Not meaning to sound conceited, dear. But if that had been the motive, wouldn't *I* have been the target?"

"Maybe they were mixed up about the drinks."

"Impossible. I never had a Pink Squirrel in my life."

"Then suppose, for some reason, I was closer to finding the murderer than you."

Frank Washington was out by the desk, drumming his fingers.

"What did she tell you?"

"Nothing. She knows nothing."

"Well, *I* know something. Analysis of Miss Peloquin's drink shows it was full of ergotamine tartrate, a known abortifacient. Any idea where it came from?"

"Certainly not."

"Listen, Matt." He held his hands up in a peace gesture. "Some people are going to presume it was self-administered."

"That's crazy! Why?"

"The lady was single and pregnant. A good enough 'why'."

"This is 1987, Frank. Abortions are legal."

"Not for her. The fetus was too well-developed. And as a stable owner, Miss Peloquin had access to the drug. Egotamine tartrate is used by veterinarians to facilitate labor." He showed me his report. "Your friend took a mare's dosage."

"Someone slipped it to her, Frank. It was attempted murder."

"All right, so we operated on that assumption. But we couldn't do much investigation on the scene. By the time the area was secured, masks removed, I.D.s made, most of the guests had scattered. Of those curious enough to hang around there was no one there who shouldn't have been."

"That's the advantage of using poison. The perp can be far away by the time it's consumed."

"So here we have a murder and a poisoning both connected to the Mayor's election."

"Not necessarily."

"And Matt Sinclair finds himself mixed up in both." Frank tilted his head back and looked down his nose at me to make much of the fact that he was taller. "You know I'm an atheist."

"How's that?"

"I don't believe in coincidences."

I found Jake at his regular post behind the bar in Pat O''Brien's courtyard. He served my usual morning Bloody Mary without cue.

"This'll be on me, Matt. I want to thank you for convincing the police those drinks were good when you picked them up."

"I saw you mix them. And Karen's first sip didn't do her any harm either."

"Someone must have loaded Miss Peloquin's drink while you were out dancing. The place was so crowded it was easy."

"Not that easy. The chemist said the compound wasn't readily soluble. It would have to be poured into the drink and stirred for at least a minute."

"Pretty dangerous to be seen doing that even in a mask."

"I'm supposing the poisoner watched me get the drinks then ordered a Pink Squirrel for himself. He had plenty of time to stir the ergotamine into his own drink. Then it took only a second to drift by our table and pull the switch."

"Yeah, that could work."

"So think hard. Did anyone besides me order a Pink Squirrel?"

His jaw dropped. "Damn! Yeah! I thought it was funny at the time. The guy who came up right after you ordered the same thing. He just pointed and said he wanted one of those."

"He? It was a man?"

Then Jake looked perplexed. "Guess so. I mean it was someone in a Ronald Reagan mask. Got the impression it was male."

"White or black?"

"White…" he scratched his head. "Or it could have been a fair-skinned black man."

"Tall or short?"

"Didn't notice that he was either. Just medium everything."

"How was he dressed aside from the mask."

"Didn't notice that either. Sorry Matt, I've already told you more than I know."

CHAPTER TWELVE
Thursday Morning

When I walked into the shop, Steve looked startled.

"Joanie stopped by and told us about Karen. We didn't expect you to come in today."

"Karen's out of danger." I walked through to the office. "So it's back to business as usual."

Steve followed. "Business as usual in greasy work clothes?"

"I didn't have time to go home." I shut the door behind us and opened my Chippendale armoire where I always keep a change of clothes. Blazer, slacks, shirt, tie, and underwear all color-coordinated.

"Then you didn't sleep either."

"I may have dozed off in the waiting room."

"Must have been very restful." Steve picked the day's checks off my desk, each clipped to its corresponding bill. "These are for Philip. Tuition at St. Boniface, vet's fees for Dickens,.. Just get a load of his farrier's bill.."

I held it at arm's length and whistled. "That horse spends more on shoes than I do. Less on hats though."

"Probably. The big bite is still coming." He handed me his pen. "Your other nephew Ronald is up to two hundred bucks on his computer resource time. Isn't he over the limit again?"

"Sure." I bent over the desk and flipped through the checks signing quickly without reading them. "But I'll let it go. Maybe this month is a fluke."

"That's what you say every month. I think you're letting Ronald run up all those bills out of guilt."

"Guilt for what?"

"Just because you favor Pip over him."

"That's true and no doubt obvious to all. But so long as I treat them the same, my conscience is clear."

Steve snapped his fingers on the itemized statement.

"Seems the computer genius has been logging in at 6:01 every weekday afternoon like clock work. And he spends all day at it Saturday."

I opened the bottom file drawer where I keep my spare socks.

"At least he waits for the off-hours."

He took the checks and a sheet of stamps. "Now, if you don't mind I'll go mail these so I won't have to hang around here and look at you nekkid."

"Go. There's too much envy in the world already."

I was into my change of underwear (filed under "U") when the desk phone rang. It was my private line so I answered it myself.

The voice on the other end was Sylvia's. Hysterical as usual.

"Matty! The most terrible thing in the world just happened!"

My heart stopped. "To Pip?"

"No, it's *George*. The bulls just came with a warrant and arrested him." She was crying uncontrollably now. I feared she would short out the phone.

"Sylvia? Pull yourself together and read me the warrant."

"The whole thing?"

"What did they arrest him for?"

"Why, murder, of course."

"What's this 'of course'?"

The explanation came haltingly, punctuated by racking sobs.

"They found the fishing knife that killed Rodger was from George's tackle box. Well, of course he had it in the back of his pick-up when he went fishing on Saturday, so who else could have swung with it?"

"What did George say?"

"He went into the Sphinx bit. He didn't even stand up for himself but just let those oinks take him away." Her voice had climbed to an ear-withering pitch. "How could he lay this on me?"

I signed off and punched Frank Washington's number. He picked up on the first ring and grunted. His mouth was full.

"All right. Where have you got him?"

I heard him chew thoroughly and swallow before answering.

"Short for 'Hello Frank, how are you this morning?—By the way, I heard my cousin George was just taken into custody. Would you please advise me on his status?'"

"Right."

"Well, I'm fine, thank you. Yes, we discovered new evidence which forced us to get a warrant for Mr. Sinclair."

"The murder weapon?"

"That fishing knife was a special issue Osborne. Some of his shop students will testify they gave one to him last semester."

"There are probably a dozen just like it around."

"But his is missing."

"Someone could have stolen it."

"The tooth fairy?—And it ties into Lloyd's 'dying message'. He could have been pointing to Sylvia, not as the murderer but as the motive."

"Listen, Frank. Lloyd was stabbed in the back and it took him a few minutes to die. An amateur job."

"Who said your cousin was a professional killer?"

"But he *was* a professional. George served two tours in Vietnam."

"I don't follow."

"He wouldn't have done such a sloppy number, Frank. He was trained to sneak up behind an enemy and cut his throat ear to ear. Instant death. No dying message."

"That'd be like putting his name on it. Is George a stupid man?"

"No. Nor a violent one."

"You're welcome as a character witness. Bail will be set in Judge Waldron's court tomorrow morning."

"I'll be there."

"You can save your gas, Matt. Your cousin has requested a public defender."

"A public defender? Why doesn't he just hang himself with a wet sheet?"

"He can't afford to hire an attorney." There was a rustle of paper over the line. "And something else you may enjoy. Neither will he take one cent from... Here's the direct quote: 'That candy-ass fag cousin of mine.' Hmm. Wonder who he meant."

"*Whom* he meant!" I tried not to slam the receiver too hard as I disconnected.

I was modestly attired at last and halfway through the payroll when Steve knocked on my door an hour later. When he opened it, his eyes were bright.

"Matt, the most beautiful, exotic, oriental doll just walked in. Floated in, I should say. Like some kind of a rare butterfly."

Then Kim glided in past him for a dramatic entrance in her double-breasted trench coat in lamb leather. I arose to pay court in the spirit of Sir Walter Raleigh.

"Enchanté, Mrs. Berber. Welcome to my humble establishment." I took her coat and gave it a padded hanger while she held onto her snakeskin purse with both hands. It was red to go with her Adolpho suit. "May I get you something to drink?"

I enjoy making these elaborate displays of gallantry to the type of woman who really appreciates them, in obeisance to that axiom: "Treat a whore like a lady and a lady like a whore."

"I'm not here shopping for furniture, Matty." She was cool as a spoon on your eye. "But if the offer is still good, I'll take a cognac."

"C'est mon plaisir." I selected a spot-free crystal goblet and half-filled it with Courvoisier. Kim sipped daintily then ensconced herself on my fauteuil, crossing her slender legs above the knees as though posing for a pantyhose ad.

She had the look of an Asian princess, soignée and exquisite. And so far removed from that hungry waif who once scrounged around an army base to survive only one day to the next in a scrap of a country ruptured by war.

There was nothing fragile about her voice or her sentiments.

"Not to waste time, I came to tell you about our connection with Rodger Lloyd."

"A connection? Your husband assured me there wasn't one."

"My husband.." Unconsciously, she grimaced at the term. "It wasn't Farley who engaged Rodger for his campaign."

"I see. Then it was you."

"I saw the need for an image consultant."

"No argument. Why did you settle on that one?"

She uncrossed her legs and let her Bruno Magli Italian shoes drop off.

"I met Rodger six years ago when we worked together on a campaign in Houston."

"I hadn't known you were in politics."

"I was in sex. They've always gone together."

"For Democrats, anyway."

"I was in charge of providing hostesses for Senator Huddle's fundraising parties."

"Is that the word? 'Providing'?"

She dismissed my interpolation with a flick of her hand, the fingernails long and red.

"I was careful to hire only Texas girls, so we never had to cross state lines. Anyhow, that's when Rodger and I became friends."

"So after Berber filed for the Mayor's race, you asked your friend to come on down to New Orleans and get your husband elected."

"I didn't kid myself that we had a chance at City Hall." She curled up in the chair like an exotic cat. "But at least if Farley could upgrade his image. Acquire some dignity.. Maybe there would be enough momentum to put him on the City Council or the School Board... We would be invited more.."

"You had it all mapped out. The woman behind the man."

"What do you expect of me? He isn't much, but he's all I've got to work with." She raised delicate shoulders. "I'll do the best I can with him."

"Did you ever consider that you have yourself to work with?"

"What do you mean?"

"Look how much you've done by yourself. How far you've come since Saigon or Bien Hoa. Where ever."

"Long Binh." she pronounced the syllables as though they had no meaning. "I'm a realist, Matt. I know I have a certain kind of cunning, but no real talent. No education or marketable skills." She finished the cognac then shook her head and put the glass down. "When I was ten years old, I discovered my single negotiable asset. The G.I.'s paid off in cartons of Salems but I was able to trade them for food for my family."

"I'm a realist too. For that time and place, you had no alternative."

"I used my femininity to buy my life, then to pay my passage to the States. And then to buy clothes, make a home.." She held her hand out to study the diamond throwing off bits of colored fire under the ceiling light. "I always understood that if I were to get anything out of life, it would have to be a man who gave it to me."

"But now you have resources of your own. Energy, industry a fine head for business.."

"All of which might get me steady work as night manager in a Vietnamese restaurant. Look around you, Matt. Those women you see down at One Canal Place buying the furs and jewelry aren't tycoons. They're the wives and daughters of tycoons." She opened her purse and drew out a carved ivory compact for a quick check of her maquillage. "It's you men who have the power and make the money in this rotten world.

"So Farley has acquired the power and the money. And it's up to you to go after the social position."

"It is." She looked weary and for a moment almost her age as she returned the compact to her purse and slipped her tiny feet back into their designer shoes. "Though right now, I'd settle for respectability."

"So would I." I helped her on with her coat and walked her to the door. "Thank you for being honest about hiring Lloyd."

"Honest has nothing to do with it." She tossed her long and shining hair. "Rodger's assistant is in town and he's been working with us. You would have found out anyhow."

CHAPTER THIRTEEN

Thursday Afternoon

"First, how's Karen," Armand called the second he saw my face. I closed the door behind me, cleared a chair of campaign fliers and sat down.

"Resting comfortably. I'll be able to take her home tomorrow."

"We sent her flowers as soon as we heard," Ed Stokes said morosely. "I know she won't be up to working on the campaign anymore."

"She said she's still willing."

Armand looked eagar for a bare second till I appended, "But I won't let her. She's retired from the game."

"Why?" Ed half rose out of his chair. "You think she was poisoned because of her association with us?"

"Maybe."

My cousin shook his head. "If someone wanted to stop us, why not just kill me? I'm accessible."

"I don't know how Karen became a target. But until I do, she'll remain isolated."

"You're right," Stokes said pragmatically. "She'd be no good to us dead anyhow."

"Thank you for your concern."

He kicked a wadded bumper sticker and it rolled into the corner. "You know what I mean·"

"I know she would have brought thousands into the treasury that's lost to us now."

Armand fanned himself with a leaflet. "We're trying to make it up from other sources. But now we're in the red for T. V spots, paper and printing." He held up his adding machine tape. "I refuse to be one of those candidates who defaults on campaign debts. No more buying on credit, and no more unsecured loans."

Ed loosened his tie a quarter inch. "You know that half our lenders don't even expect to be repaid."

"Don't kid yourself. Those power brokers count on getting their money's worth one way or the other. The day I'm sworn in, they'll be knocking on my door for appointments,..city contracts,.. No!" Armand threw down his pencil and it bounced. "I'm not that kind of politician. Have we exhausted all sources of no-strings contributions?"

Ed groaned. "With this stock market thing, everyone is pulling back on support. Good luck to us."

I said, "All the political action committees have reported in except Gay PAC. But they're behind you."

"Tell them thank you and I'll take whatever they have. I'll also accept with gratitude any canvassing they want to do on my behalf. Homosexuals are very civic-minded."

"We have to be. If we don't work to form social policy, we become the first victims of it."

Ed raised a finger. "There's still one Democratic fat cat whose tail we haven't pulled. Dick Dickerson hasn't taken sides."

"Dickerson?" Armand tasted the name and shook his head. "He's a multi-millionaire all right, and devoted to politics. But he votes the conservative line."

I said, "He registered as a Democrat because it was the only party in the state till ten years ago. He's also known as a white supremecist."

Armand said, "Then there's no chance he'll come in with us."

Ed cocked his head. "There is if your lilly white cousin over there strokes him a little. You game, Matt?"

"I volunteer. To be as white and as persuasive as I can be in the name of the cause."

"You can persuade him if you can find him," Armand suggested. "Dickerson owns Juno Foods, one of the biggest concerns in the state. But I've heard he's never in his office."

"That's common knowledge. So I expect to catch him at his secondary enterprise."

"What's that?"

"Speculating in relative equine velocity."

CHAPTER FOURTEEN
Thursday Afternoon

Robin was bouncing in the right seat.

"Here I've been living in New Orleans three years and this will be my first time at the race track."

"I've been neglecting it too. Basically I'd rather ride horses than bet on them."

We have two tracks in the area with consecutive schedules for racing all year long. The food and the ambiance are usually better than the horses or the jockeys, but an aficionado like myself can enjoy an afternoon of shrewdly placed bets and modest winnings in comfortable surroundings.

The lot usually isn't crowded on a weekday, so we were able to park directly in front of the club house. I paid for admission and programs and led the way up the escalator.

"Remember we're only staying two hours. I have to run back to the office."

"Mr Dickerson is sure to be wrapped up in his betting." Robin called to my back. "Why don't you catch him when he's doing something else?"

"Dick Dickerson is *never* doing something else."

We passed through the restaurant between banks of empty white tables to the left and full ones to the right. Corporation parties and charity affairs had taken various sections for the afternoon. We made our way down the stairs to the best tables, right in front of the wall of windows with a panoramic view of the entire track. My man was easy to spot, a tall and robust Texan with prematurely white hair. "Whenever he's in town, Dick conducts every business day right there."

It was almost one o'clock, post time, and Dickerson had set up housekeeping at his usual table by the far stairs. He was poring over the *Racing News* and didn't look up till I'd taken the chair beside him and asked for a menu.

"Hi Matt. What do you think of Hickory Doc?"

"By Woodman out of Doctor's Daughter. Good blood."

"Yeah, I know this horse can run. But it's only a five thousand dollar purse." He tapped the paper. "Does the owner want him to run? Is the jockey gonna let him run? What do you think?"

"I have no inside information."

"But look here; he's on bute. I *know* Locksmith is going to come in. I'd bet the family jewels on him."

Robin settled in across the table and studied his program.

"Ooh, Matty! Yellow Ribbon! Isn't that an adorable name?"

Dickerson wagged his pen. "He's a dog. Ran out of the money last five out of five starts."

"But I love yellow."

"Go ahead and bet him," I pushed a five dollar bill across the table. "It'll be a lesson in prudence."

Dickerson pushed over a twenty. "For the Exacta: Number two and number nine. Box 'em."

Robin performed his usual mime of total non-comprehension so I translated. "Go to the Special window and bet two to win and nine to place. Also bet nine to win and two to place."

Robin repeated these instructions several times to digest them before scampering back up the steps to the betting windows.

Dick underlined the "Pick Of The Day" in his racing form. "Who do you like in the Trifecta?"

"Actually, I didn't come to invest, but to meet you in your office here."

"That so? Well, my secretary must be on her coffee break. What can I do you for?"

"I'm working for Armand Voitier in the primary."

He looked skeptical. "Don't tell me I should put my money on that ol' boy for mayor."

"He's the chalk in a three-horse race. You can't get better odds out here."

Dick pushed aside his salad plate, leaned back in his chair and looked me over as though I were a cob of unknown pedigree.

"Just what would I be gettin' for my stake?"

"Your own way."

"That so." He pushed his lips out and folded his program to the next race. "Don't try to kid a kidder. Voitier wouldn't be throwin' any city business my way."

"He wouldn't have to. Armand is doing more than anyone else to increase the tax base of the city. He wants to give incentives to big businesses to stay in the area. Who's going to profit? Concerns like Juno foods."

The color television above us announced that the horses had reached the starting gate. Robin ran outside and down the steps to root for the horse with the cute name and I could see him through the window jumping up and down and waving his arms.

Dick, by contrast, was so jaded that he didn't bother even to look out the window but watched the race on our T.V. monitor, nodding passively at the progress around the track. He stopped watching before the horses had turned into the homestretch.

"And the winner is: Yellow Ribbon way out in front!" proclaimed the speaker. "..Harry's Boy, Pot O'Gold, Bye Bye Now, Abdication, Friendly Tom, Hickory Doc and.. *Locksmith!*"

A minute later, Robin bounced back inside, flushed with victory. "Ooh, my horse beat all the others! What do I do now?"

Dick was tearing his tickets into confetti.

"You prance on back to one of those little windows and collect your winnings."

"Hey, this is fun!"

And the lucky fool ran up the stairs waving his ticket.

My companion uncapped his Mont Blanc and circled the number three. "What do you think of Lady Night going off at seven to one? Finished in the money last five times."

"Good odds. I knew her when she was a foal. She likes to run." I scanned the program. "And she's never been on medication, so her condition must be good. She doesn't have a fast time on the morning line. But that stable never exercises them full out."

"Plus this jock is good, but he hasn't had a decent purse in two months. I don't figure he's going to pull her up."

I pointed with my chin to a fat and happy looking couple settled by the window. He in a heavy gold nugget watch and she in sable. "And the filly's owners are sitting right over there. I think they'd like to get a picture in the winner's circle."

"Me too." Dick reached for his wallet. "Like to cow?"

"Why not? Put me in for twenty. Win-place."

This was the way to bet scientifically. Know the horse, know the jockey, and know the owner. Check the morning line, and analyze the odds.

Robin rejoined us, breathless and flipping through a roll of new bills. "Guess what! I thought I was only going to get ten dollars. But that guy gave me a whole *hundred*!"

"It was twenty to one odds," I informed him shortly.

"What a great way to make money."

"We're going to make some now," Dick said. He pushed my twenty and one of his own across the table cloth. "Half to win and half to place on the number three horse, Lady Night."

My "significant other" looked shocked. "But Matty! A horse named 'Robin's Pride' is running in this race. How could you not vote for him?"

"Her. It's a ladies' race. Anyway, names have nothing to do with speed. Robin's Pride always fades in the stretch, and we have the longest stretch in the country."

Dick snorted. "Little buddy, that horse is so slow, she wears lights on her head so she can find her way in after dark."

Robin squared his shoulders which could use it.

"Well, I'm certainly going to bet on my own name!"

"Go ahead. Invest our money and waste your own."

When the trumpet sounded, I stood up at the window to watch the start. I was able to sit down again ten seconds later.

"The number three horse, Lady Night, has thrown her jockey going out of the gate," the speaker blared.

"I told you she likes to run," I said glumly. "You have to admire her enthusiasm."

"Consider it admired." Dick held our tickets so it was he who had the pleasure of tearing them up.

"But the race isn't over yet." Robin insisted. "Your horse might come in first."

"I am sure she will. But it doesn't count unless there's a jockey on top of her."

"Oh."

When "Robin's Pride" won by a length, nothing was said by any present.

After the next race, Dick had himself a well-marked program and a pile of shredded tickets at his feet. He finished his third Rusty Nail and ordered a fourth.

"My luck can't be *all* bad today. Tell you what, Matt. I'll listen to your political spiel."

"Thank you."

"Along with those of the other two candidates, just to be fair. I'll invite Moses Jones and Farley Berber to send any spokesmen they choose to represent their own positions."

"You're talking about a three-way debate?"

"Nothing so structured. More like an intelligent discussion among the civic minded. Y'all come on out to my place in Beaumont Friday and make a night of it." He regarded his program ruefully and put it aside. "Anyhow I'd like you to check out the new stallion I just bought."

"Delighted," I said without stopping to consider, because I hadn't any choice.

CHAPTER FIFTEEN

Thursday Evening

I was just in from the track and seriously attacking my work when Steve interupted me.

"Matt? There's a young man outside to see you. Stranger. Yankee too, going by his accent."

"A tourist?"

"Hmm.. No plastic name badge. No Bermuda shorts or polyester flowered shirt.. Toting a brief case instead of an Instamatic.." He shook his head. "I would say not a tourist."

"I'll take him."

The lithe young not-a-tourist sauntered through the door, shifted his eel skin brief case to his left hand and held out the right. "Mr. Matt Sinclair?"

His "Matt" rhymed with "sad". It didn't take a dialectition to figure that he was from the mid-west.

"Nolo contendre." I hurried around around the desk to meet him because natural courtesy is bred in my bones and because, fortunately, this Yankee's A's were the only flat thing about him. His teal business suit was European-cut and the trousers were just tight enough to show off an unbusinesslike lower torso. His hair was strawberry blond and waved as though it had been Marcelled.

"I'm Raymond Harris." (Rhymed with "heiress".) "Lieutenant Washington said maybe we could help each other."

"And what a brilliant incisive man he is, Mr. Harris." (I rhymed it with "Paris".) I shook his hand, holding it longer than customary for the standard introduction and wondered how Frank knew it was close to my birthday.

Mr. Harris seemed confused and blushed slightly.

"I was referring to the investigation of Rodger Lloyd's murder. The lieutenant said you know as much about the crime scene as anyone else and I about the victim. So perhaps we ought to pool our knowledge."

"Happy to jump in the pool with you." I opened the door to my office refrigerator, an antique Victorian ice box modernized with a new motor and condenser coils. "How about something to drink? Hard or soft?"

"Oh, thank you." He looked past me to the stock. "That orange juice would be nice."

"And would complement your coloring too." I shook the bottle till it foamed and poured him a crystal tumbler full in tribute to his peachy skin and green eyes. I put the glass in his hand, touching his fingers, and showed him to the fauteuil.

Young Mr. Harris placed the brief case primly on his lap and tried his orange juice. He assessed me over the glass rim as I perched on the edge of my desk.

"You're definitely a 'winter-romantic'."

"Pardon?"

"Your type. We classify people according to different color seasons. Your rose beige skin and dark hair make you a winter."

"I know about color seasons. We keep the charts and swatches around so we can personalize a customer's interior decor."

"But we also go by the 'clothing personality' types. You're not striking and authoritative like a 'dramatic'."

"I'm sorry."

"You're too sensual to be a 'classic'. And of course not nearly masculine enough for the 'natural'."

"Dearie me."

"So you're a 'romantic'. You've got that artistic flare, the soft curly hair with just a touch of gray... The arresting eyes.. The good proportions.."

"Thank you from the bottom of my proportions."

"And your clothes reflect a tactile nature. The cashmere blazer, fitted at the waist, pleated trousers in pearl gray.. Just exactly." Then my new pool mate lowered his lashes and smiled shyly. "Gay, right?"

"Right and left."

"I knew it." He crossed his legs and finished the juice. "Straight men have no eye for color and style. That's my business."

"Color and style?"

"Exactly. I was Rodger's media image expert."

"Ah, so! You helped his candidates primp for the video cameras?"

"You make it sound silly, but basically yes. When a client called us in, Rodger would analyze his strong and weak points in reference to the district's political climate then write his speeches and commercials. My job was the man's appearance. Looks are important, you know."

"Indubitably. I'm enjoying the hell out of yours."

"Thank you." The compliment made him sit up and preen. "They say Richard Nixon would have been elected in 1960 if he'd had a better make-up man for the debates."

"Indeed." Mr. Harris had probably said all this before and was saying it again.

"And answer honestly. Do you think Ronald Reagan would be President today if he didn't dye his hair?"

"He denies it."

"Phoo. I'll bet he uses Nancy's. They do it when they're all alone at the ranch late at night so no one catches them."

"Perhaps. Certainly, I have the greatest respect for your profession, Mr. Harris."

"If you're not going to say it right, I wish you would just call me Raymond."

"Delighted, Raymond. I've read that your firm is responsible for clinching several close elections."

"And a few considered hopeless. Rodger was one of the top ten in the country. Some candidates called to see if we were available before they even filed. Berber was lucky to get us."

"No doubt. There's hardly a man more desperately in need of your services."

"I've been working with him intensively since I flew in and already filmed commercials with his new image. You'll see the difference a little expertise can make."

"I'm looking forward to them. Tell me what you know about your late employer."

The peach color of his cheeks deepened to a light coral, revealing an intention to tell less than he knew.

"Rodger was a very brilliant and difficult man. Recently our work had changed the course of many elections and he was proud of his new power and prestige.

"Quite a successful man then."

"In some ways."

I was alerted. "How about financially?"

Raymond shifted in his chair as though trying to make it fit him. "When a man is paying off two ex-wives and keeping four daughters in expensive schools, he doesn't have much left to put into the firm." His tone was guardedly bitter.

"Or to pay salaries?"

"The past two years, I've been working for half what I was worth. Rodger promised that when we had won a few elections and proved ourselves, he would be able to give me a partnership. A share in the profits."

"Which never happened."

"And I deserved it, Matt. There was never anyone more loyal. I put my heart and soul into that business. He just wrung every ounce of energy out of me."

"The more I learn about Lloyd, the more he seemed to need killing."

"That's true." Then he looked up, startled. "But, geez, *I* wouldn't have done it. I'm too much of a coward. —Could I have some more orange juice?"

"You can have it all." I reached over for the bottle and handed it to him, letting my hand rest on his. "What do you think of Lloyd's so-called 'dying message'? He was found with his face on a book of Audubon plates."

"That was in the papers." Raymond poured only a dainty

half-glass.

"Did it mean anything to you?"

"Hardly. Rodger tried to interest me in ornithology. He thought it helped to characterize our clients and their opponents as birds."

"Like Berber?"

"He said Berber looked like a buzzard, but we were going to make him over into an eagle."

"Very clever."

"Moses Jones was a crow, of course."

"What else?"

"And he saw Armand Voitier as a penguin because he's so formal and uptight."

"Did he ever liken any candidate to a garden warbler?"

"Oh, I see what you mean. No. And not a cuckoo either." Raymond opened his briefcase. "But Rodger was a recognized expert on all kinds of birds. He wrote articles for magazines like *Bird Watcher's Digest*. I brought the last one he published in case you're interested."

Birds interest me a little less than Ed Meese's sex life, but a thorough investigator investigates thoroughly.

Raymond handed me the magazine turned to the beginning of the lead article but I skimmed ahead.

"..The wood version of this species can be distinguished by its brown-flecked breast and employs the most elaborate system of communications." Lloyd had written. "Within a two-day period, I personally observed one male sing his entire repetoire of calls from the mellow D above high C of his mating song all the way up to an urgent staccatto warning cry a full octive higher."

I was in danger of falling asleep sitting up.

"How fascinating. I guess the man really knew his..birds."

"He treated them better than people. Had more regard for them at least. Like to keep the article?"

"If you don't mind. —When did you last speak to Lloyd?"

"He called me last Wednesday. Three nights before he was killed.

"Did he mention any enemies he had here?"

"No. All he could talk about was his son."

My heart skipped. "His son?"

"Rodger said he drove out to St. Boniface and saw him in the school yard. He didn't approach him then because the boy was with his brother."

"A name? Did he tell you his son's name?"

Raymond moved his head negatively. "Just that he expected to catch up to him when he was alone."

"But he never did."

I heard Steve's "shave and a haircut" knock on the door. Knowing what I had inside, he was too discreet to barge in.

"Matt? Do you still want that staff meeting at five-thirty?"

"Sure, bring them on." I opened the door and turned back to Raymond. "How about further discourse over dinner?"

"Oh?" He had been expecting and awaiting the invitation but was yet coy enough to hesitate. "If you think we might make progress."

"I know I will." I got the name of his hotel, showed him to the office door and shook hands warmly. No more than that because Steve was watching every move with arms folded.

At Raymond's departure, I hustled back to my desk and the phone. "Just give me a minute to make a reservation at Kitt's."

Steve only smirked as is his wont. After nine years working for me, I think the smirk has set into his face like a coffee stain.

"I knew you would like that kid, Matt. He's the same type as Robin: short, blond, and blooming."

"Young Mr. Harris is nothing like Robin. He has something between his ears besides whipped cream."

"Then I'm sure Robin won't mind a bit that you're spending the night at Kitt's with a *sensible* person."

"He'll never know. I'll just call home and tell him I have to work late, and that I'll be sacking out here on the sofa bed. That's what I'll tell Robin."

"You've been telling him that about once a month. I don't think he's believed it yet."

I reached in my pocket for a ten dollar bill. "Here. Send Gary out to get me some of those sheepskin jobs."

"You think they're as safe as the others?"

"Hmm. You may be right. Better stick with the latex. But tell him not to bring back those stupid-looking colored things. I felt like a clown last time."

He looked down at Hamilton's picture. "How many do you want?"

"It's only for one night, so a dozen ought to do it."

"You're bragging."

CHAPTER SIXTEEN

Thursday Night

Kitt's Club, behind its spear-topped iron gate, is the most exclusive establishment in South Louisiana and the least publicized. Membership is entirely gay, and in the interest of privacy no straight people are allowed anywhere on the premises on any errand or pretext.

I bring my dates here to enjoy the nineteenth-century decor, to bask in the romantic atmosphere and to revel in the scintilating company of like-minded souls. And there's Kitt's cuisine which rivals anything on the Continent. (We hired our chefs away from Maxim's.) And then at the close of the evening one may partake of the amenities of the third floor.

The sight of two grown men checking into a hotel together would be too disgusting to consider even in New Orleans. And I can't exactly bring a new amour home to Robin.

As we took our seats, Didi, my regular waitress, already had my drink mixed and she tottered over to deliver it on stiletto heels. I'd known her before her operation when she was still Danny and had liked her better that way. But then I think any man gets a distressful feeling in his groin at the prospect of another offering himself for castration.

Didi seems not to regret her choice though and cherishes her surgically wrought womanhood as only a convert can.

"First your Sazerac." She leaned in low to serve it, showing off her C cup siliconed accoutrements. "And what would your young friend like?" Her false lashes fanned him. "Afraid we don't serve anything as yummy as he is."

"No chef is that good. Raymond is an orange juice man."

"With Vodka this time," my date amended.

Didi pursed her crimsoned lips and said slowly. "A screw-oo

driver, I'll squeeze it fresh just for you."

"Just the oranges. I hope you don't have to squeeze the potatoes," I allowed. "We don't need the menus. Bring us oysters for the appetizer. The freshest topping, whatever it is."

"He just made the cheese sauce."

"Bienville then. And etoufez the crawfish. Salad with the house dressing." I turned to Raymond who now looked peeved.

"Trust me."

"I'd like to at least pick my dessert if you don't mind."

"Our first lovers' quarrel. All right, kitten what do you like?"

"Apple pie?"

"Nothing so middle-American mundane here. Bring my friend the apple charlotte, Didi. And if Ben Gruber shows up, will you ask him to join us?"

"Ben's in the restroom probably showing it off. If he ever comes out, I'll send him over." She wiggle-walked back to the bar, checking over her shoulder only once to assure that I was still watching.

Raymond looked around shyly. "If every one in this place is gay, can we hold hands?"

"Absolutely."

"I've never done that in a restaurant before."

"This is *our* world here."

He reached for my hand then abruptly dropped it when we were precipitiously intruded upon.

"Hey, Matt?" It wasn't the awaited Gruber who interupted but another, sadder, club member. And he descended on us like a dark angel, flapping a large-format magazine. "Got something to show you!"

Dennis Quinn's suit hung in folds, while his shirt collar gaped away from his scrawny neck. The wretch was losing weight faster than he could buy new clothes in smaller sizes. Not that he would get any wear out of the new clothes either.

I managed to convey light-hearted enthusiasm.

"Hey Dennis! Please sit down with us." I quickly introduced my date and reinforced the invitation by pulling a chair back. Dennis bent and slid into it, his knees collapsing in the last second before his bony rear hit the seat.

Even so, he looked happier and more bouyant tonight than I'd seen him in months. Or since he'd found out.

"Look here Matt." He spread out the magazine. "Did you read the new issue of *Spin*?"

"Not likely." I noted the picture of Sting on the cover. "Isn't that some sort of teenage record tabloid?"

"Usually it's just about music. But there's a vitally important article this month."

Raymond studied the newcomer tactfully with averted vision. No doubt seeing the haggard ashen face with its irregular peach-colored patches of Covermark and wondering what they covered.

Dennis handed me the issue already folded to the relevant page. "There's this new formula they invented in Israel."

I scanned the article and Raymond read the title over my shoulder. "AIDS: Words from the Front."

Then he looked back at Dennis and came the dawn. His eyes grew wide and frightened as though this were his own death he beheld.

Dennis hunched over the magazine. "See, this formula was developed by the Weizmann Institute in Israel and they call it AL 721. Do you understand? The cure is already perfected!"

"Perfected?"

"The substance isn't toxic like AZT and it'll be available for one-tenth the price. It's all right here in black and white!" His hand quivered on the page. It was discolored with purple blotches of Kaposi's Sarcoma. "One man was too weak even to move or speak. He had to go to Israel in a *wheel chair*. But they gave him this stuff now he's leading a choir in Hoboken!"

Raymond looked startled. "Hoboken?"

I had to be gentle. "Dennis, if this is really the cure, it would be the scientific breakthrough of the age."

"Yeah, right. Here it is!"

"Then why isn't it on the front page of the *New York Times* instead of buried in a kid's record magazine?"

He rotated his shoulders inside his suit. "The big papers should pick it up any day now. *Spin* broke it first, that's all."

Didi delivered Raymond's screwdriver without a word then race-walked back to the bar, not caring to be drawn in to the conversation.

Dennis underlined the title with a fleshless finger.

"It's been tested on thirty-four people and thirty-three are still alive. Isn't that proof positive?"

"Still alive after how long?"

"A whole year. This stuff is made out of egg yolks and it kills the virus."

Raymond was staring openly now. "Just egg yolks?"

"Sure. Anyone can make it if he only has the formula."

"The magic formula," I said.

"Not magic, modern science. The answer is right here!" Dennis's eyes were fiery like those of any fanatic who had to believe in something unbelievable. "Of course it's secret. But this small company in L.A. has the patent and now they're waiting for FDA approval to sell it as a drug."

"That could take forever."

"But there's a lot of pressure to approve it. AL 721 could be available to the general public within a year. Just you wait and see."

"I hope you're right, Dennis."

"Sure, sure. And I'll be the first in line at the drug store too." He glanced down at his hands then self-consciously pulled his sleeves down to cover the blotches. "Soon as I'm back in shape again, I'll give the biggest bash this place has ever seen. You're invited!"

I executed some sort of smile and squeezed his shoulder.

"You can bet I'll be there."

"Great! Yeah!" Dennis picked up the magazine and folded it carefully. He made to rise from the table and was successful only on the second attempt. "I'm gonna spread the word. *Everyone*'ll want to hear this!"

Raymond and I sipped our drinks in silence. After a few for-tifying swallows he breathed, "Egg yolk now?"

"Ginsing, rhino horn, Laetril, fetishes and incantations... Now it's egg yolk. Why not?"

He knit his brow. "But what if that AL 721 is the honest-to-god cure?"

"What if?"

"And what if that rinky-dink company in L.A. takes a year to get the thing approved and put it on the market?"

"What if again."

"Has Dennis got a year?"

"You kidding?"

Ben Gruber finally came to meet us carrying his can of Dixie, no glass, and carefully selected a chair other than the one just vacated. We all turned briefly to watch Dennis unfold his magazine and break his earth-shaking news to a table of architects across the room. Then Ben rotated his chair so he wouldn't have to see anymore.

"He's been showing his pathetic magazine to everyone who walks in the door. Like if he can get enough people to believe in it, maybe it will come true. That poor guy gives me the creeps."

"He could be any one of us," I reminded.

"Don't I know it? Five of my good friends are dead and maybe a dozen more like Dennis."

"Ben, this is only the beginning of the plague. I heard there's one block in Faubourg Marigny where every single apartment has a case."

"I'm gonna start wearing my rubbers two at a time."

Ben Gruber, the chairman of the gay political action com-mittee, is a tall, muscular hunk of a florist whose head is shaven like Mr. Clean's. He tipped the Dixie, judged it low, and sig-naled Didi for another.

"Say Matt, if you called me over to ask about Armand, the Gay PAC has collected over eight thousand for him." He raised his can in a toast before draining it. "Tell your cousin we'll either endorse him or curse him out, whichever he thinks'll do him more good."

"Why him?" Raymond addressed Ben's pectorals. "What has Voitier done for the gays?"

"Voted to knock out the sodomy statutes in the state Senate. Voted for more money for AIDS research and treatment. Voted to outlaw job and housing discrimination on the basis of sexual orientation."

Didi placed Ben's Dixie in front of him without the nicety of a glass and lingered for an affectionate pat on the rear which he delivered off-handedly. "Yes, Voitier's our candidate."

"But that other black man, Jones, must be the more liberal," my date interposed.

Didi snorted, an unlady-like holdover from her boy days, and appropriated the vacant fourth chair in a shocking dereliction of duty.

"Moses Jones only sees black. He thinks he's a liberal but has no understanding of gay issues."

"My guest here needs re-educating," I told him. "Raymond has been making commercials for Farley Berber."

"Forget that wacko!" Ben appropriated my fork to beat rhythm accompaniment on the crystal flower bowl. "He takes the straight conservative line. Berber wouldn't even meet with our representatives. Claims homosexuality is aberrant and he won't condone it as an alternate life style." He aimed the fork at Raymond. "Your client would drive us all back into the closet."

"As if you ever saw the inside of a closet," I said.

Ben Gruber is the only man I know who has appeared in gay porno films under his real name. He suffers from a serious shame deficiency.

"I meant 'us' in the general sense."

"I may not agree with Berber's ideology." Raymond stirred his screw driver which had separated into two layers. "But I'm bound to do the best I can for him."

"I hope you're not too ego-involved with the campaign. Berber is so far behind the others he can't even see their tail lights."

"We've discounted him as a factor," I advised.

"Even if he did well it wouldn't mean much." Raymond sucked his straw. "After all it's just a primary."

"*Just* a primary?" Ben choked on his beer. "That's Voitier's best shot!"

I tapped my date's knee. "You're only a Yankee, so I'll give you a quick overview of New Orleans politics. About half our voters are white and half black and they're pretty well polarized."

He nodded. "That's true in most cities, nowadays. In Philly it was like fifty-one/forty-nine. The blacks for Wilson Goode and the whites for Frank Rizzo. It's hard to get a coalition."

I held up one pedantic finger. "But New Orleans history has given us a unique natural coalition."

Ben groaned. "Uh oh. Don't let Matt get into one of his famous history lectures."

"Because New Orleans history is Sinclair history too." There was no stopping me. "My six-times great grandfather, Artur St. Clair, immigrated in 1745 when the French Quarter comprised the entire settlement. Since then there has always been at least one Sinclair living within the city limits."

Raymond didn't even pretend to be impressed. "But what do your ancestors have to do with present-day politics?"

"Back in colonial times, most European settlers of means took black slave women as mistresses."

"The white ones were lousy lays," Ben interjected.

"And when a slave women presented a Frenchman with a son, the usual custom was to free them both. So there emerged a new stratum: free men and women of color."

"Who were fruitful and multiplied." Ben waved his hand in a circular motion, speeding the narrative up to its conclusion. "So we've got us a whole class of people who aren't white but then they aren't black either. And Armand Voitier represents the best of them."

Raymond frowned. "I should think the mulattos would be out-numbered on both sides?"

"They are," I said. "But if Voitier just makes the run-off, he's got to be our next mayor."

"How do you figure that?"

Ben took up the lecture. "If Voitier faces Moses Jones in the general election, he'll be the whitest man running. So he gets the white vote and the middle class blacks. Shoo in."

Didi pulled on his arm. "On the other hand, if he runs against Farley Berber, Voitier gets to be the blackest man running. So he inherits the black voters and the white liberals. Easy win."

Raymond pondered the lesson. "I think I get it. You're afraid that Moses Jones will gobble up the liberal black vote in the primary. Then if Farley gets all the white conservatives, your man Voitier will never make the run-off. Right Matt?"

"Now you've got the picture. In that case it would be even money on the other two as in Philadelphia. White against black. Fifty-one/forty-nine."

My date smiled like a Delilah with scissors in one hand and Sampson's pigtails in the other.

"So that's our agenda. In order to keep Berber in the race, we've got to knock over Voitier."

Didi's eyes flashed. "Matty, how could you have brought this viper into your bosom."

"You wanted him in your own bosom, a minute ago. —Give me the key."

She got to her feet and leaned forward, allowing me to extract my room key from its usual cache in her cleavage.

"But don't rush upstairs now. Your dinner will be out here in a minute."

"We'll wait for the dinner."

"Not me." Ben chug-a-lugged his beer and stood. "I'm rushing upstairs. And I'll use two rubbers. So long Matt."

"Good luck. Uh.." I called after him. "Who's your partner?"

"Ain't bringin' one!"

Raymond's eyes were wide. "That's *very* safe sex."

"Ben used to be the wildest man in the club too. I remember when he entertained seven admirers from Jackson Barracks in one afternoon. Four enlisted men and three officers."

He patted his hair. "I was never in the service. But I remember running into Ben somewhere before. Or is it just wishful thinking?"

"He's sort of a movie actor. They say he starred in the famous classic, *Tom Dickin' Harry.*"

"Oh, that was a fabulous film. I saw it."

"Well, I didn't. And I don't even want to know whether he played Tom or Harry."

CHAPTER SEVENTEEN

Friday Morning

I awoke when the sun stabbed my eyelids. Pulling the pillow over my face, I realized both that I was on the third floor of Kitt's and that I had forgotten to close the skylight before falling asleep. I did so now, groping at the bed-side control panel. This particular sinner is never ready to acknowledge a new day with all its promise and responsibilities before a jolt of strong coffee.

In time I sensed that someone was beside me with whom I had probably committed several crimes against God and the State of Louisiana. But I wasn't yet willing to plumb my fuzzy brain for a proper name.

"Say, kitten?" I spoke through the pillow. "That phone there will get us room service."

"Not yet, Matty. It's just almost that time." I uncovered my eyes to observe Raymond rise from the bed, sans breeches. He padded across the Persian rug to open the Edwardian server that camoflaged our jarringly anachronistic TV set.

"Time for what?"

"They told me eight-oh-one: channel six." He pushed the power button with a peachy toe and the screen blinked on. "Our new commercial."

The setting was the Lake Pontchartrain levy and in the foreground stood Candidate Farley Berber, rugged and windblown, in his green plaid flannel shirt and khaki pants while his cordoroy McGregor jacket whipped around him.

"New Orleans is a vital and growing city," he told the camera with forceful sincerity. "And we're going to make it grow in the right direction.."

"This is the sixty-second version," Raymond said. "How do you like it?"

I rolled out of bed. "Incredible."

I was indeed awestruck at the metamorphosis of that gangling yokel astride a saw horse into this credible "outdoorman".

The candidate spread his spidery hands like a conjurer about to make something wondrous appear out of thin air.

"We'll bring new business to this region to increase the tax base and furnish jobs for our unemployed. We'll cut waste in city government and put that money into the education system for our kids..."

Svengali was bouncing with excitement.

"I banished all his suits which just made him look skinnier. Plus they were *all* the wrong colors. I mean he had nothing decent in his wardrobe. I had to roughen his image, so I sent to L.L. Bean for new clothes and had them shipped Federal Express."

"Brilliant." I reached past him to push the "record" button on the VCR. It would only get the last half of the spot. But that would be enough to scare the bejesus out of Armand.

"You see, Matt? What he needed was that macho 'man-of-action' look and I think I've achieved it, don't you?"

"You've achieved more than I would have thought possible."

Raymond hugged his knees. "The record already proves that he's a successful business man, so there's no need to stress his brain power. We just have to show the voters of New Orleans that he's a *real* man. You know what I mean?"

"You have your work cut out for you."

"I styled his hair myself, giving him sort of a woodsy look with a blow dryer and half a tube of mousse." He traced Berber's outline on the TV screen. "The make-up was easy except for that awful nose. It took me a half hour to contour the thing so it looked natural."

"If you run enough of those spots, the voters may forget his 'Park yore horse 'n' rig,' commercials."

"That's our fervant hope. Trouble is, we're out of funds."

"Out?"

"Well, Farley has put up as much as he can afford without mortgaging his whole enterprise. The money from the Republicans is used up. And anyone who would like to give out of the goodness of his heart has given his limit. People contribute to campaigns because they expect to reap some benefits of the victory. No one likes to back a loser."

"He won't be able to buy more TV time."

"Afraid not. But if our man makes a good showing at the debate tonight, we could get into the race." Then he snatched a hand to his mouth. "Yipe! I shouldn't be telling you all this. You're the enemy!"

"Very true. But if you want to grab the menu. I'm friendly enough to buy you breakfast."

It was almost noon when I got back to the house for a change of clothes. Robin didn't meet me at the door as customary but remained planted on the living room couch and pretended to read a magazine. I knew he was pretending because it was The New Yorker.

"Hi, Kitten."

No answer. Then I realized that he was giving me the silent treatment which I should have welcomed as a vacation. But it was mine to make at least a token attempt to mollify him.

"Are you unhappy about something?"

"No!"

"Good."

He threw down the magazine. Hard, so the pages fanned and it closed itself.

"Why should I be unhappy just because you lied about staying in the shop all night?!"

How did he know? How *much* did he know?

"Well, not all night. You may have called when I popped down to Felix's for some oysters."

"Felix's?" He sprung to his feet. "I happen to know you were at Kitt's. And with someone *else*."

"Who told you that?"

"I just know!"

I had long suspected Robin of having a secret ally at Kitt's. Some patron or employee who would flounce off to the phone anytime I acted in a manner unbecoming a husband. But there was no use in trying to extract the mole's name.

Femmes are just like women. They make up a covert network of spies and sabateurs covering every place and every walk of life.

"But, Kitten!" I put my arms around him. Angry or not, he still felt warm and smelled agreeably of V.O.. "I only lied out of respect for your feelings. I didn't want to upset you."

"Thanks a whole pant-load!" He pulled away, turned his back and declaimed to the wall in a manner reminiscent of Doris Day's "outraged virgin" films. "Just last week you and I had a long talk about our relationship. Didn't it mean anything?"

Talk about "relationships" almost never means anything at all, and I certainly hadn't listened to that one but I said, "Of course it did."

"Did you forget we promised that we were going to be faithful to each other from now on?"

"Faithful? Well, I *am* when I possibly can be. That thing at Kitt's last night was business." I took off my cashmere blazer in pearl gray and handed it to him automatically and he accepted it automatically.

"You mean the dude *paid* you?" He headed for the bedroom and I followed him.

"He was Farley Berber's campaign manager. I got a lot out of him."

"Ooh, I'll just bet you got every *drop*. Anything comes along in tight trousers.."

"How did you know about the trousers?"

".. you forget I even *exist*." He stomped over to the closet and flung its louvred door aside so violently that I winced. "I've loved you and *only* you since the day we met. I haven't even *looked* at another man. And you treat me like dirt!"

"You're the one I come home to. Doesn't *that* mean anything?"

"It means you want a *slave* to pick up after you, wash your underwear and cook your stupid Cajun recipes, that's all it means."

He selected a wooden hanger and arranged my blazer on it, equalizing the weight of the shoulder pads. Then he wheeled around and assumed the classic soap–opera stance of confrontation: chest out, chin lifted.

"Three years ago, I gave up a *career* for you."

"And for that I've always been grateful."

His "career" had been picking up tricks in the lobby of the Roosevelt Hotel, but to point that out would have been ungallant.

I took off my shirt and tie and he snatched them.

"But in all that time, you've never shown you loved me in any meaningful way." The tie went back to the tie rack, the shirt to the laundry hamper.

"Tell you what, Kitten. You're just depressed because winter is coming. This afternoon, why don't you trot on down to One Canal Place and buy yourself a new wardrobe. A few angora sweaters should make you feel better."

I pulled my T-shirt over my head and he caught it, mid-way to the floor. "Buying me clothes doesn't mean anything. They're eef.. eef.." He threw his arms up. "They don't last!"

"Ephemeral."

"I don't want angora. I want to feel loved and needed!"

"I love you as much as I reasonably can. Hand me the navy pinstripe."

He took the suit from the closet and thrust it at me. "Show it, Matty!" My white linen shirt was still packaged from the laundry and he lobbed it over like a frisbie. "Show the world!"

"That's preposterous."

"All it takes is a simple walk down the aisle. Simple words: 'I will.' People who love each other do that."

"Not two *male* people, for pity's sake!"

"I want a 'convenant of partnership' ceremony. No money,

no sweaters.." He held out my red grenadine tie like a garrotte. "Let me know when you've decided!"

Then he tossed me the tie, marched into his own room and closed the door to begin a boycott á la Lysistrata.

I dressed quickly, unassisted and not terribly concerned. One disadvantage of youth is the overwhelming sex drive. A man of my vintage can hack celibacy longer than any kid.

CHAPTER EIGHTEEN

Friday Afternoon

An hour later I replayed the Berber ad to an attentive audience at my cousin's headquarters.

Armand removed his steel-rimmed glasses but the situation looked no sunnier out of focus. "God, he's become a viable candidate." He waved at the TV screen. "If I didn't know better, I'd vote for that man myself."

"We've been throwing all our ammunition at Moses and ignoring our right flank." I re-wound the video tape. "Last week Berber's constituents were mainly racists with a fourth grade education. Now with this kind of positioning any reasonable conservative might listen to him."

He sighed heavily. "Let's face it. This isn't our week. First Karen gets sidelined as cheer leader and we lose our lock on the uptown set. And now they've got a feasible Republican in the mix."

"But.." Ed Stokes groped for a hopeful note. "You said his campaign doesn't have the money to run these."

"Said my source. But if Berber shows a chance of getting City Hall, the money will come."

Armand left his chair and began pacing. "If I were Farley Berber right now, I'd go around to the fat cats who were holding back before and show them that tape."

"He's way ahead of you. Tonight he'll be debating you and Moses Jones on live TV. And bet he'll be wearing his 'new look', contoured nose and all."

"Maybe he can't debate."

Ed spoke to his chest. "What does that matter? All he has to do is stand there and look good and be white.

The Forum For Good Government sponsored the evening's

debate, the last televised showcase for the candidates in the UNO University Center Auditorium.

I could have gone backstage to watch the contest or sat with Armand's faction. But I picked up a yellow legal pad and planted myself in the midst of the audience to feel as well as hear their reactions.

All three candidates passed the first test which was to sit up straight on stage without fidgeting or leaving their shins exposed. Then a Professor of Political Science explained the rules of order and congratulated each and every one of us for involving ourselves in the democratic process.

Moses Jones lost the coin toss so he came to the podium first to give his opening remarks in the rhythmic emphasis of a revival preacher or a rap artist, punctuated with rocking shoulders and a thrown fist. He postulated that the Mayor of New Orleans could and must work to alleviate the problems of the black community like truancy, crime, and unwed motherhood. He neglected to mention that these crises were all brought about by internal moral dissolution which no mayor had any power to dispel. But his constituancy were out in force endorsing every exhortation with heartfelt "Amen"s and "Yeah, you right"s throughout.

Armand was next up, standing straight and tall as though for military inspection. His dispassionate speech about luring industry to the area with more technical education and tax incentives produced many good points but failed to inspire. The people around me began to murmur among themselves about where they would go for seafood afterward. I wrote "zzzz" on my legal pad.

Farley Berber was the last to speak and all his years of hawking portly jeans on TV hadn't gone for nothing. It was with surprising eloquence that he revealed himself to be dead in favor of goodness, daily prayer, and a return to traditional values. That these precepts had nothing to do with city government was beside the point in a world that had elected Ronald Reagan to the highest office in the land on an even vaguer platform. My seatmates listened to him and nodded as though their acceptance of his rhetoric could take us all back to a simpler time.

Halfway through Farley's address, I spotted Raymond Harris in the back of the auditorium coaching with barely perceptible hand signals. Slow down.. speed up.. Louder.. Quiet.. He made a subtle fist and a second later the Republican banged his own on the podium for a very effective bit of business.

Next on the program was a period of questions from the audience. Of course the candidates didn't actually answer the questions posed but used one as a jumping off point for a pre-rehearsed mini-speech. Jones mildly rebuked Berber for not caring enough about the disenfranchised poor. Berber, for his part, gently suggested that Jones was a bleeding heart liberal with no practical plan to finance his social programs.

Neither mentioned Voitier at all but pointedly addressed each other over his head. I wondered if there were actual complicity in this tactic or if the liberal and the conservative decided independently to treat their middle-of-the-road opponant as the man who wasn't there.

To top off the evening, the Forum had laid out a buffet in the rear of the auditorium. This was ostensibly an opportunity for informal chit-chat with the candidates but was actually a "spin" session. Campaign workers assailed newsmen and commentators with reports of what had really happened up on stage lest they believe their own ears.

"Farley Berber made the best showing tonight," declared Ollie Dunn from the Republican State Central Committee. "Because he's bringing the people of this city what they want. A return to old-fashioned values." Warren from News 8, a black man, nodded politely and didn't betray what he was thinking.

A prosperous-looking black union boss had button-holed Lynn from TV 6. "New Orleans is part of the 'New South'," he declared. "We could gauge by the response that Moses Jones has a new ground swell of support among white voters."

Our own Ed Stokes had captured Angela from Eyewitness News. "Armand Voitier is the only candidate who broaches substantive issues. And the people appreciate that he doesn't represent a 'cult of personality'. Just solid good government."

Way to go, Ed. When our man has (Let's face it.) no discernible personality, we try to turn his blandness into a virtue.

Millie from the *Times-Picayune* stayed apart from the fray, sitting on the sidelines and jotting away on her steno pad. I casually took the chair beside her and tried to read it.

"Spying, Matt?" She smiled and showed me the page. "Do you read shorthand?"

"Not Gregg.—But let me tell you what really happened up there on stage."

She laughed, her dark eyes disappearing into new-moon squints. "Never mind 'spinning' me. I'm just doing a soft feature on the candidates' wives."

"I can help you there too. Claudia Voitier has an MSW degree. She's an exemplary wife and mother of four who devotes all her spare time to various charity endeavors."

"Fashionable charities," Millie pointed out. "New Orleans Symphony, the Opera Guild, Friends of the Zoo,... Mrs. Voitier is quite photogenic too, in Teri Case coiffures and size-ten Perry Ellis. Our paper has a file on her thicker than the phone book."

"I can't add much to that."

"Mrs. Moses Jones, on the other hand, is the choir mistress of her Baptist Church, uses a hot comb and shops at Catherine's. Not chic or sexy but popular with working-class blacks."

"Popular with me too. She's real."

"The big story, if I could write it..." Millie underlined a shorthand curly-cue. "..would be Mrs. Farley Berber. She's beautiful, exotic, mysterious..."

"And one smart fortune cookie."

"Right." She waited for me to say something. When I didn't, she said it. "I am aware that Mrs. Berber was a high-priced prostitute."

"Um.. Hunh?" It being incumbant on me to play very dumb at this point.

"And before that, a *low*-priced prostitute."

"Please, Millie. Don't even hint at her background."

"You're a gentleman?" It was a question.

"Considering the make-up of this city, if Berber cops the prostitute vote, we'll never beat him."

"Prostitutes don't vote. They're night people. Anyhow, I couldn't play with Kim Berber if I wanted to. The *Times-Picayune* is a family newspaper."

"You could damn with innuendo."

"Just make much of the fact that the woman's past isn't discussed? If I hated her I would.—I don't hate anyone."

I found Raymond standing by the table with a paper plate of non-descript edibles. "Campaign food," he picked up something unrecognizable with his plastic fork. "Not so appetizing as K-rations, but it keeps us going."

"Congratulations are in order. Your man made a fine showing tonight."

"Thank you.—Do you think this is chicken?—Rodger wrote the speech. But the image was my creation."

"Your good work may just get Berber elected Mayor of New Orleans."

"Why Matty, you flatter me."

"Think about it."

CHAPTER NINETEEN
Friday Night

When I got home to Esplanade Avenue after the debate, my windows were dark which should have alerted me. Usually by this hour, all the lights were on, heaters were blazing in every room and Robin was curled up on the sofa in his pajamas watching *Knott's Landing*. When I let myself in, the rooms seemed worse than dark and cold. There was a heavy unfriendly stillness around me. I walked back to the bedroom to hang my jacket up myself. And then my heart pounded.

The closet was half empty. All of Robin's clothes were gone.

So the little queen was running a bluff on me. He thought he could force me into his humiliating "covenant of partnership" ceremony by hiding out somewhere for a few days.

I wondered where. Not that it mattered.

The silence of the house was so thick now that it was hard to breathe. In an attempt to alleviate it, I turned on the stereo expecting to hear JOY 102, but it had been switched from the FM to the record turntable. And Luther Van Dross's rendition of "A House Is Not A Home" came woofing and tweeting over the speakers:

> *I'm not meant to live alone.*
> *Turn this house into a home...*

Our song. Robin had done that on purpose.

I flipped it off without troubling to lift the needle and Luther slowed down to a bass before shutting up.

I lit the gas heaters, cooked my own dinner which I can do better than Robin any night of the week, then flopped into my recliner to watch the tube. Ted Koppel wanted to talk about

AIDS so I played a tape of *Frank's Place*. It's a treat to see a program about New Orleans that doesn't resort to unlikely voodoo practitioners or grainy Mardi Gras footage.

I watched my old neighbour, Fran Roberts, play a scene in Hollywood's version of a New Orleans restaurant and wished the French Quarter were really that picturesque and artfully lit. And that we could all live our lives in soft-focus under star-filters.

I had no trouble at all finding my own pajamas and turning down the bed. I had grown used to Robin after three years but certainly didn't need him.

I lay with my eyes open till the clock struck one then turned on my reading lamp. I reached for the telephone and punched Kitt's Club.

The Maître d' called Didi to the phone and she answered too casually.

"Hi, Matty? Want to make a reservation?"

"At this time of the morning? Come off it. Where's Robin?"

"Gee, how would *I* know? He's *your* lover." The tone said, "Which you seem to have forgotten, to your peril."

"No games. I want him back."

"Well... That's up to *you*, isn't it?"

"Just tell him." I hung up.

If Didi wasn't harboring Robin, she surely knew who was. All those femmes support one another.

I felt *dépaysé* which in French means exiled and in Cajun means just plain miserable. I got up, poured myself a glass of milk and added some brandy to it before tackling sleep again.

I had no special need for that particular little queen over any other with the same general qualifications. It's just that it felt natural to hold him in my arms on a cold night. More natural than not to.

A shadow of my usual self showed up at New Traditions the next morning. It wasn't open for business yet, so I let myself in with my key.

Steve Hicks rose from behind a Queen Anne-style settee and

flapped a handful of sale tags.

"Hey Matt? Good debate last night."

"Apf? Unh."

Then he made the mistake of looking at me.

"Geez! what the hell happened to *you*?"

"No sleep again last night."

"Those circles under your eyes would do justice to a coon."

Steve was going to find out sooner or later, so I told him the truth. "Robin walked out on me."

"Why in hell would he do that? You were supporting his little ass."

"I'll say I was. Fine restaurants, charge accounts, cash allowence... There's nothing he couldn't have. Do you know of any wife who's been treated better than that little airhead?"

"Nope. Nope. How long have you two been together?"

"*I've* been together a good fifteen years. Robin has *never* been together."

"No, but.." Steve put down his price tags. "I guess you..uh..want him back?"

"I guess so." I shrugged. "Sure."

He dogged my heels all the way back to the office.

"I don't know how it is with your faction. But when a woman leaves a man, she's either, A., through with him or, B., trying to force his hand at something."

"It's B.—I need some coffee."

"I just made some fresh. Well?"

"Well, I hope it's hot."

"Well, what does he want?"

I reached for my Saints "Who Dat?" cup. It wasn't clean and I didn't care.

"Promise not to laugh?"

He crossed his heart. "Hope to die."

"He wants to marry me."

"Umph! Umph!" Steve made a manful try at keeping his lips clamped but finally gave up and doubled over into a rolling, sputtering, har-dee-har.

"Stick a needle in you eye, sport." The coffee was too hot to drink but I wouldn't compromise it with milk.

"Hoo Hoo!" He fell on the couch still rolling and pointed. "Hey, Matt? Ca..Can I be your best man?"

"You can be my best unemployed man if you don't stow it."

But he couldn't or wouldn't. "D..Doesn't he have to promise to raise your children as Catholics?"

"Naturally it wouldn't be a conventional wedding. What he wants is a gay 'covenant of partnership' ceremony."

Steve managed to gaffaw himself out and sat up.

"I've heard about those. So are you going to walk down the aisle with him?"

"I'd sooner be dragged down the aisle, naked and on fire."

"Okay, stick to your guns. You can always get another kid to warm your bed."

I ignored that unwelcome bit of sensibleness. "What Robin wants really is a sign of committment. Legal and binding."

"That's marriage."

"There are other means. I've had all night to think about this. All bloody night." I tasted the coffee which was good, I having roasted the beans myself over the weekend. Then I knelt and twisted the dial of my floor safe.

"Steve? What's the combination?"

"My birthday, remember?"

"Yes, I remember that the combination is your birthday. But I forgot your freakin' birthday!"

"Shame on you. Two-seventeen-forty-eight. I'm an Aquarius."

"Congratulations." The thick fire-proofed door swung open on my first try. My papers were all neatly catagorized and stacked. "I'll call Buddy, my insurance man, and have a policy drawn up with Robin as beneficiary."

"Good idea. That'll fool him."

"I'm not trying to fool him." I pulled out the relevant papers and kicked the door shut. "He ought to have some security in the event of my untimely demise. I'll issue the policy to Robin and let him pay the premiums so the benefit won't become part of my estate."

"Then he won't have to wait for probate. OK, but you're a relatively young man. Maybe he won't like waiting forty years to collect your little token of love."

"He won't have to. He's also getting this." I tossed Steve the legal-sized packet from the safe and he unfolded it.

"This is the deed to your house."

"For a simple title transfer. I want Jean to type it up in legal form."

"You're giving away your home?"

"Not the whole thing. If I put his name on the deed along with mine, that will give him the legal and binding partnership he craves without the embarrassing spectacle I abhor."

Steve re-folded the deed.

"That's still very generous of you."

"He's been with me almost three years. The lad deserves some sign of appreciation. And tell Jean his real name is Robert Fischbach, Jr.. In case something happens to me, I don't want him to lose out on a technicality."

"When do you need this for?"

"Tomorrow is soon enough. Then I'll send it by messenger to prove my honorable intentions."

"Hello, uncle?" It was Pip knocking on the door jamb, his eyes bright with anticipation. "Am I too early?"

"No, come right in. I'm glad your mother is letting you come."

"Mom likes me to hang out with you. Dad isn't so crazy about it, but he can't argue now." He lofted his overnight case over his head. "I can't wait to take off."

"Ready here too. The car is gassed up and you get to drive all the way to Beaumont, Texas."

"Fantastic!"

"It's a straight shot on I-Ten. And I'll be sound asleep most of the time."

"I don't mind. Hey, why are you wearing jeans instead of riding clothes?"

I picked up my wardrobe bag. "I'm a born diplomat, Pip. Our host is pure D. Texan, into the Ponderosa look, so I wore jeans and packed jodhpurs. When he invites us to go riding I'll be prepared for western or English."

"What are you going to wear if he chooses bareback?"

CHAPTER TWENTY
Friday Night

Dick Dickerson had deployed his money in all the traditional outlets of business and pleasure and still had a few million left over. So he decided to start up an equine veterinary hospital for a state-of-the-art horse health care center cum tax-shelter.

The hundred and forty acre D.O.D. horse farm boasts a surgical suite, intensive care unit and the most advanced research techniques. But I go for the riding where a man and horse can gallop miles through green meadows without meeting a wall or fence.

Pip pulled into the drive smoothly and parked beside a two horse trailer with the D.O.D. logo. I freed myself from the seatbelt as Bob's wife Linda, fetching in a prairie skirt, separated from a milling lawn party and sprinted over to meet us.

"Hello, Matty. We've just had some neighbors in for lunch. Sorry you missed it."

"I'm sure they were well-entertained without me."

"Could be." She glanced around at the hearty group composed mostly of rich horse breeders in Texas-style semi-formal with gold belt-buckles and string ties. "The other political factions have beat you here."

Taking her hand, I spied Moses Jones, clad in his usual urban finery, his custom-tailored three-piece suit accented with a gold watch chain. He waved and a cuff link glinted under the fading Autumn sun.

"Hi there, Matt," he called. "I was here first with the most."

His cordovan leather shoes were shined to a high polish which he futilely tried to preserve while stepping around the yard frequented by horses.

"He who laughs last, Moses."

I introduced my hostess to Pip who carried my bag as well as his own in his aide-de-camp role and Linda tactfully greeted him as an adult.

"Are you in charge of the luggage, Philip? Let me show you upstairs."

"I'll unpack us, Uncle," he assured. "You can stay down here and talk politics."

"I look forward to it. All points of view being duly represented."

My nephew followed Linda into the house swinging the bags to make them look light and I turned to our third political spokesperson.

If there were anyone less suited than Moses to life on a horse farm it was Kim Nguyen Berber.

The little oriental flower, exquisitely dressed as always in a St. Laurent suit with a short, tight skirt, picked her way across the yard in three inch heels. On reaching me she clutched both my arms to keep her balance.

"Hi Matty. Welcome to the wild west."

I scanned her, head to toe and back again.

"You're not going riding like that."

"Have you ever heard of an oriental who rides?"

"No, I haven't. Then where is your rodeo aficionado husband?"

"He won't get here till after dark, when it'll be too late for riding."

"Really? What's the delay?"

"Off the record?"

"Sure."

She stood up on her toes to whisper and her Opium perfume came up with her. "Because that buffoon is scared of horses. He was thrown during a trail ride when he was twelve years old and never got back on."

"I promise I won't tell," I said softly enough so the approaching Moses wouldn't hear.

"I trust you." Kim checked the bottoms of her shoes for

damage. "At least no one will expect me to get up on one of those things."

"You look like china in a bull shop around here. How do you get along with the Texans?"

"Business as usual. They're all johns. They look. They wink. They brag.."

"Let them brag," Moses interjected. "I helped three of 'em brag this afternoon and got three good donations."

However inappropriately dressed, the man was operating in the spirit of the occasion and I congratulated him.

Kim looked past me and smiled. "Ooh, what have we here!"

Pip had unloaded the bags and was on his way back down the terrace. She nudged me. "For something like that, I would forego my customary fee."

"My nephew, Philip. Fifteen years old."

"Just the right age."

The party seemed to be breaking up as our host, Dick Dickerson, bid his luncheon guests goodbye and came to meet us. "Hello, Matt." He slapped my shoulder. "Feel like jumping tomorrow?"

"I was hoping you'd ask. I'd like to do the full course at least once before breakfast."

"We've got a chestnut gelding named Joseph who will fit you like a custom saddle. Good manners. He's a little on the lazy side but I think you can get him to move."

"My specialty is motivating slow horses. I hope he's an early riser."

"You'll never know from me. I don't even look out the window till ten. Want to introduce you all to my newest baby in the east paddock."

Pip frowned. "A baby?"

"A baby horse."

"Oh. That kind I can appreciate." And he ran ahead of our host all the way down the path to the equine nursery. I gave Kim my arm so she wouldn't break one of her impeccable ankles in the rough turf. Moses of the shiny shoes was careful to reconnoiter every step he took.

When Dick leaned against the rail, Pip settled beside him in the identical posture to admire the new baby.

"Get a load of a real beauty, Mumtaz." Dick pointed fondly. "Both parents were Derby contenders. This little girl is only five weeks old and already running for the roses."

Mumtaz was running around her paddock on long spindly legs, enjoying her new life, her young strength and the October wind in her mane.

"Perfect confirmation, great spirit, top quality," I observed. "Could be you've got another "Genuine Risk" on your hands."

Then the filly stopped to nurse from the only other horse in the paddock, a short-legged broad-crouped mare.

Pip hung over the fence raptly. "She's just the wet-nurse, right? That old nag couldn't be Mumtaz's mother."

Dick laughed. "That's what I brought you all here to demonstrate. The foal's genetic mother is Princess Iris, winner of the filly triple crown. But her brood mare is Molly there. 'That old nag.'"

"Now I see the light. Embryo transfer."

Pip cocked his head. "How's that?"

I was able to give him the facts as explained in *Horseman Magazine*. "The breeder takes a fertilized egg from a great mare like Princess Iris and transfers it to a utility brood mare. That way, the superior mare can produce several offspring a year without losing time from her career as a race horse."

"A surrogate mother?" Pip was incredulous. "I thought only humans did that."

"But the mare doesn't give the foal back at birth. She thinks it's her own and raises it herself."

"Old Molly isn't much to look at," Dick conceded. "And she couldn't outrun any one of us. But you can see she's a first rate mother."

Molly had turned her head around and was nuzzling the young derby contender over to a more promising teat.

Moses clicked his tongue. "Indeed, we must preserve the genetically superior at any price. I'm glad they didn't have this science a hundred and fifty years ago. They'd have made black women bear and raise white children."

"I won't argue the ethics of surrogate motherhood, but there's plenty of precedent in nature," Dick defended. "Some species of bird does it habitually."

"Ducks are negligent *couveuses*," I said, "So back on 'Nonc Aldus's farm, we used to sneak duck eggs into the hen's nest."

Moses looked dubious. "When they hatched out ducklings instead of chicks, didn't the hen feel ripped off?"

"Not at all. She thought they were her own babies. I remember how she'd line them up, march them around the barn yard and teach them to scratch for food."

"She didn't get suspicious when they started quacking?"

"Not then, but when the little ducklings trotted into the pond to swim, poor mother hen would flutter around the edge of the water squawking with mortal fear."

Dick leaned over the rail and laughed. "Adoption is universal." Now the plain old mare was encouraging her beautiful young nurseling to gallop and even trying unsuccessfully to keep up with her. "Molly has given me five foals already. Every one of top racing blood. The finest traits will be passed on."

Then Kim said her only words on the subject.

"Isn't the trait of being a good mother one worth passing on?" With that, she turned heel and walked back to the house.

Farley Berber arrived in time for cocktails, wearing a designer buckskin jacket which actually became him. Raymond must have been dressing him for social as well as public appearances.

Dinner in the main house of the D.O.D. horse farm would have done credit to Ben Cartwright and sons. Hop Sing himself couldn't have brought off a better pork roast. The corn bread was made with fresh-that-morning eggs and milk. The greens were out of Linda's garden and bowls of fresh butter went around the table.

All throughout dinner, our host held forth at the head of the table, telling jokes and urging extra helpings. But he didn't formally address the company until the dishes had been cleared. Then he pushed his chair back and stood ceremoniously.

"Linda and I want to thank you, our political guests, for favoring us with your company this evening. Now we're going to excuse the ladies while we enjoy our after-dinner brandy and cigars."

Linda and Kim jumped up as though freed by a dismissal bell.

"We'll rejoin the gentlemen after they've done making themselves sick on those nasty cigars and polluting the room with tobacco fumes," Linda said sweetly. And she linked arms with Kim for the exeunt.

Not craving a lungful of smoke either, I myself would have preferred to follow them out. But such wasn't my mission.

Pip though was "in his plan" as the Cajuns say, exhilarated at being included in this company of men. He put both hands down and took a firm grip on his chair as though afraid of being ejected from it.

"The floor is open while we pass the cigars around," Dick invited. "It should make for lively and entertaining discussion of the issues."

Farley said, "I'll be happy an' proud to give you my own personal views on everything, Dick." The Hispanic maid placed a silver humidor on the table in front of him. He eyed the assortment and selected a corona, rolling it between his hands. "An' I notice Mister Jones there ain't afraid to do the same."

"Oh, Ho! What have we here?" Dick picked out a Royal Lonsdale. "Subtle underhanded thrust from the far-right? Matt can you parry?"

"My cousin Armand is equally happy and proud to make his views known." I didn't care for a smoke. "Unfortunately though, he can't do it on horseback. That's my province."

"Touché!" Dick put his cigar in his mouth and used both hands to applaud. "For the record, I don't penalize Mr. Voitier for not coming himself. He has an excellent emissary in Matt."

"I'll debate you under the table tonight, Farley," I exchanged a look with Kim. "Then I'll ride you into the ground tomorrow morning."

"Hanh?" He concentrated on the lighting ritual. "Actchully, I cain't take you up on that."

"Much as you'd like to."

"Much as I'd like to, cuz I got to high-tail it back to New Orleans right after breakfast. Bidness."

"Sorry about that," Dick said generously. "And you Mister Jones? Will you be riding with us tomorrow?"

Moses lit his panatella, cupping his hand over the end and puffing expertly for a cool and even burn.

"I'm afraid I'm unable. You see, I was born in the ghetto, brother. There were no horses in my neighborhood. I didn't even have a bicycle." He waved the cigar "no". "The poor black children of New Orleans never had a chance to participate in that most wholesome sport, I'm sad to say. I used to work after school as a groom in Audubon Park, combing and saddling the horses for white people to ride. I was not permitted to ride myself. No sir." The panatella went back into the mouth and was puffed rightouesly.

Here was a brilliant way to turn a liability into an asset and I admired his tactic. At the same time I recalled that Moses Jones's father and grandfather were ministers in one of the wealthiest Baptist churches in the state. If he never owned a bicycle it was because he preferred riding in the new Cadillac his father bought every two years. And whatever he knew about being poor and black in New Orleans, he'd learned from hearsay.

Pip oh-so-nonchalantly selected a cheroot from the cigar box. I shot him a look fraught with meaning and he just as nonchalantly put it back.

"I'm well-armed to talk about ideology," I said.

Dick let an ash drop into a receptacle carved of volcanic material. "Suppose we talk about politics instead. Government is politics, right? Before and after the election—Farley?"

Berber stiffened to attention.

"Farley, two weeks ago, I wouldn't have given a cow chip for your chances. But you looked damn good in those new commercials."

"I thank ya for yer encouragement."

"But I'd have liked to see an expanded campaign. Too bad that Lloyd fellow got himself killed."

"We been workin' without him," Berber said tersely.

"But with his speeches and his game plan, right?" There was no reply. "Right." Dick pointed his cigar at Moses. "You've got a very effective campaign with complete saturation. Your machine has reached every man and woman who's likely to vote for you and convinced everyone you're liable to convince."

Moses nodded into his tie. "Yeah, we've done a good job."

"But you still haven't got your plurality. That's bad."

I raised a finger for attention. "Voitier has the plurality."

"That he does. Today. But losing Miss Peloquin's active support will cut into his numbers with the white voters. The front-runner more than anyone else has to watch his back. Our friend to the right is.." Dick walked his fingers along the table cloth. "...sneaking up on you."

The maid came back around with the after-dinner brandy. This time I let her serve me. "What you're saying is that each of us has his plusses and his minuses. A chance to win and a chance to lose."

Moses made a V of his fingers on the edge of his brandy glass. "A time to sow and a time to reap."

Berber proffered his so the maid wouldn't have to bend.

"A time to mourn and time to dance. Tell you what, Dick. Why don't you just support the candidate you would like to *see* elected?"

Dick leaned forward to tap Berber's lapel. "Because it goes the other way, Farley. Any candidate I support is sure as Hell the one I want to *see* elected."

I said, "Ideology be damned. He wants to back the winner."

"And I will."

The maid came back and filled Pip's glass with a delicious amber liquid. Apple juice. I made her a discreet thumbs up sign and she smiled and returned to the kitchen.

"That's enough of politics for awhile." Dick took the floor

again. "Let's talk horses."

Pip looked transported. "Oh, let's!"

"Here's a good story for you. In the Houston Thoroughbred auction last month, I met the most beautiful chestnut stallion in three counties. Flaming Brand by Brand Name out of Firefly. Blood lines are champions six generations back. And you'll never guess the asking price." Dick challenged us all. "Guess!"

Moses and Farley were studiously concentrating on their cigars so I did the guessing.

"For the get of Brand Name? An easy $200,000."

"Try eighty."

What's the catch?"

"That's what I said. So I checked his lungs, legs, teeth. Even had my own vet look him over. Seemed to be no catch." Dick tilted his chair back. "Anyway, this was such a fabulous animal, I had to test him out. So I rode him a few times, just around the paddock. That was my mistake."

"I see. A bad actor?"

"Loco, I think. Listen to this: second day home, I was just taking him out for a little exercise on the south pasture. Asked him for a nice posting trot. The slightest squeeze of the knees, nudge of the heels, right?" He put down his cigar and waved both hands. "This crazy horse took off at full gallop!"

"With you on top?"

"What do you think?"

"The critter wouldn't have had *me* on top long," Berber offered bluntly.

Dick coughed, shook his head, and waved smoke away.

"I stayed in the saddle, O.K.. But damned if I could guide that horse for anything! Picture all my two hundred and ten pounds pulling right rein and still couldn't turn that animal's head."

I asked, "Had Brand got the bit between his teeth?"

"No, he just didn't feel the steel on his mouth, or didn't care. That stallion is purely crazy!"

"I'd have left."

"Sure, Matt, but here's the sticker. We were running up on that stone fence over the rill. I knew it was in our path but the horse couldn't see it. And he was crazy enough to run right into the thing.—You see my predicament."

Pip nodded, "If you just bailed out you could lose the horse."

"Right. And if I didn't, I could lose both of us."

Farley coughed. "Well, don't leave us hangin'. How did it end? What did you do?"

"Once I saw that big mother-lovin' wall coming straight at us only ten feet away, still couldn't turn the horse, so I finally gave up and threw myself off."

Pip was transfixed. "So what happened then?"

"Broke three ribs."

"No. I mean to Brand."

Dick leaned back and laughed. "Spoken like a true horseman. Boy after my own heart." He sobered slightly. "Well, you'll never believe this. But that loco stallion came up on that wall and didn't even slow down. He just up and jumped the five foot wall nice as you please."

I was on the edge of my chair. "Took it clean?"

"And he'd never been trained for jumping."

"You showed good judgement, Dick. If you'd stayed on top I'm sure the horse couldn't have taken that jump·"

"No way. But he still would have tried. I agree."

Pip thrust his chin out. "I'd have turned that horse. Oh, sir! Let me ride him, please!"

"Sorry, son. No one's gonna ride that horse. He's too darn dangerous."

Farley was watching his smoke disperse around the chandelier. "If he was mine, I think I'd make dog food out of the critter."

"That'd work down to $350 a pound for dog food. Nope." Our host sipped his brandy. "First thing: I'm gonna look hard into the pedigree to see if insanity runs in the family. If it doesn't, at least I can keep him for stud."

I sided with my nephew. "If you can cure Brand's bad habits, he'd make a prize jumper."

Pip's eyes were bright. "Turn him over to me, Mr. Dickerson. I'll make a gentleman out of him in one season. —And then bring you home a wall full of ribbons.

"Coming from a Sinclair, that's a tempting offer. I'll take it under consideration."

It was nearly midnight. The moon was full which affects some people adversely, pulling on their bodily tides and impelling them out into the streets to commit bad manners and mayhem. But this was my favorite time of the month, as night my favorite time of the day.

I sat alone on the back porch looking over the pastures. The other houseguests elected to stay warm indoors but I wanted to be outside and cold and awake.

As a cloud drifted between the moon and me, I heard the steps of another night bird. Kim Berber came out wrapped warm in a full-length Blackglama mink.

"Still up, Matt? Almost everyone else has turned in and passed out."

"I can't sleep. I admire this wholesome country life all right, but I'm still on decadant New Orleans time."

"Me too. The original city kitty." Kim curled up in the chair beside me, kicked off her shoes and tucked her feet underneath her. "I wish I were home right now. The whole trip has been a bust for us."

"How do you know?"

"My 'lord and master' gave the entire content of his speeches at the dinner table and that took him about four minutes."

"Whereas most politicians have almost ten minutes' worth of material."

"I know it's all a matter of personality and thank God that boy Harris came in to make our commercials. But let's face it. Without Rodger Lloyd to write his speeches, my husband hasn't got a snowball's chance."

"Did you consider discussing his platform? A man like Dickerson is predisposed to favor conservatives."

"But Dick wants to appear to be liberal. So if he can support a Democrat without hurting his business, he's going to do it." She stretched out. "That eliminates our friend Moses. He wants to raise corporate taxes and welfare benefits, so he's just wasting his time out here. Unless he came for the country air."

"I don't imagine."

"But a moderate industry-conscious Democrat must look good to Dick."

"That's one for our side."

"And the social strata can't be discounted. You're of Dickerson's class, and so is Voitier. You've got him tied up in a bow."

We heard some commotion upstairs in the nursery where Linda was cooing her youngest back to sleep.

Kim spread her toes, polished in crimson, and was silent for a long moment. Finally she said, "I would have been a good mother."

"Do you ever miss yours?"

"My what?"

"Your baby. Remember?"

"Oh, that." She looked remote. "That was Clerow's baby not mine."

"You carried it."

"I did what I had to do to get into the country. But all during the pregnancy, I felt as though I were carrying a package for someone else."

"A novel viewpoint."

"You would understand if you had seen it.. black, with kinky hair. There was nothing of me in that kid."

"It was easy to leave him behind then."

She tilted her head as though annoyed with a particularly dense pupil. "Matt, I had to leave my *real* family behind in Long Binh. They were my own blood, my mother and sisters. I dream about them still, exactly as I last saw them, waving me along down the road."

"Where are they now?"

Stupid question. In that second, her eyes shone and her lower lip trembled. It was the first hint I'd seen of any emotion in this woman.

"No, I'm sorry," I said quickly but of course it was too late.

CHAPTER TWENTY-ONE

Saturday Morning

Pip had been given a room to himself, so he wasn't awakened when I finally turned in.

A man sleeps most soundly and effectively in the country. I awoke without an alarm in the gray dawn and pulled on my riding clothes. Before breakfast I would have the trails to myself. And in the cool hours of the morning my designated mount, Joseph, was wont to be his most ambitious.

The household wasn't stirring yet, so I met no one on the way downstairs and the paddock was empty.

Walking into the stable, I encountered no living creature except softly nickering horses and was prepared to comb and tack Joseph myself. But the stable hands must have been alerted to my early morning foray because the chestnut was already outfitted and waiting in the cross ties. His name "Joseph" was etched in the saddle leather so there could be no mistake.

I had expected my mount to be something of an old plug so was surprised at the beauty of the animal. I stepped back to admire his star racing confirmation and shining red coat.

He was as eager to go as I, tossing his mane in anticipation of the exercise.

I didn't see the groom to thank him, so I checked the girth and the nose strap, adjusted the stirrups and led the animal along the aisle way.

Lazy horses usually need a little physical incentive, so I picked a crop out of the umbrella stand by the door before swinging aboard. I was guiding Joseph out through the paddock when a Latin stable hand called Pancho came around the

barn with a shovel and a bucket. He waved at me and I waved
back. Then he looked frightened, held out his bucket and hollered:

"*Para! Para! Ese caballo es el loco!*"

The words blew around my ears as I nudged my mount into
a fast trot and then my fuzzy early-morning brain finally delivered the English translation:

"Stop! That horse is the crazy one!"

But it was too late to turn back now. Once we'd reached the
freedom of open space, the horse (Dick's notorious Flaming
Brand, of course, not the torpid Joseph) reared up into a
almost verticle posture then came down hard and bolted into a
dead gallop.

I didn't have time to be ashamed of not having known a stallion from a gelding but just dropped the whip and got
organized, shortening my reins and straightening up in the saddle. Keeping my seat was no problem. barring low-hanging
branches, I knew I could stay with this horse till he ran himself
out, but there was no guiding the animal. I tried pulling the
right rein to turn him in a tight circle but enjoyed as little luck
as Dick had. Brand didn't seem to feel the bit. If he ran in the
wrong direction he could kill us both. Mainly me.

My gut tightened to a hard knot when I realized we were
headed in the same direction the horse had traveled so tri-
umphantly before. Toward that same stone wall. If I bailed out
like Dick and settled for a few cracked ribs, Brand might make
the jump successfully and might not. If I stayed on, he almost
surely wouldn't.

Keeping in mind how much Dick would blame me if I let the
horse careen to its destruction, I took a crazy chance. In riding
academies they told us how to turn a horse who doesn't
respond to the rein but it was always a theoretical problem and
I hadn't known of anyone who'd accomplished this at a full gallop. But the wall was only thirty yards away and it was my turn
to try lesson twenty-seven.

I threw myself forward on the horse's neck, held on for dear
life with my left arm and reached around to his mouth with my

right. Then I pulled the rein right at the bit itself and working that close had sufficient leverage to turn his head. Ten yards short of the wall he veered right. I sat back in the saddle as he slowed to a canter and then to a defeated trot.

"O.K., you win." he said.

I felt like swinging out of the saddle, kissing the ground and leading him back to the barn but that would be rotten horsemanship. One must never reward bad manners by getting off and giving the horse a break. I kept a sadistically tight rein on the return leg.

Apparently Pancho had raised the alarm, for an audience of some dozen were waiting in the paddock. The stable hands, my host, and all the other guests lined up like a spelling bee, watched my progress with clasped hands and open mouths.

Dick strode forward, at once angry and relieved, and took Brand's rein.

"Matt, are you suicidal? I know you're a first-rate rider, but I told you Brand is loco."

I pulled out of the stirrups and slid to the ground. My knees almost didn't hold my weight.

"I'm a believer too, Dick. But I thought this was Joseph when I got on."

"How? Can't you read?" He made a quick examination of the horse before turning him over to a groom. "All the stalls are plainly marked."

"Brand wasn't in his stall though. He was in the cross-ties, tacked and all ready to ride."

"But no one is permitted to ride him. Geez, he has Joe's saddle and bridle on. How'd this happen?—Pancho?"

The stable hand who had tried to warn me too late and in the wrong language only shook his head.

"*Yo no comprendo nada de eso, Señor Dick*. I never touch this horse today."

"Then who put the tack on him?" No answer. Dick made a three hundred and sixty degree turn to the entire company. " I want to know what dung-brain took Brand out of his stall and left him in the cross-ties."

Kim Nguyen Berber had wrapped her arms around herself looking very cold in the brisk morning air.

"Someone who wanted to kill Matt Sinclair."

Pip was silent and white-faced as he followed me back to my room. When I collapsed into a chair, he took the one opposite and pulled off my riding boots for me.

"Do you believe what Kim said, uncle? That someone was trying to kill you?" His voice wavered as though it hadn't quite finished changing.

"What motive would any of these people have to off me?"

"None, I'm sure." But he didn't look sure at all as he carefully wiped the dust off my boots and stood them in the corner. "Unless one of the other candidates is scared of your helping Armand."

"The most I can do is raise a little money. Hardly worth risking a jail term."

"No, it's not. But then how did you end up on a dangerous horse by mistake?"

"There must be a simple explanation." I ruminated for a few minutes then snapped my fingers with it. "Suppose one of the stablehands was told to tack the big red one for me and he misunderstood. Maybe he's illiterate and couldn't read the signs. The man wouldn't own up later because he was afraid of losing his job."

Pip grinned in relief. "That must be it. Sure."

There was a single knock on the door and Dick's voice calling, "Matt? I've got to talk to you."

Pip opened the door for our host and discreetly closed it behind him.

Dick was wearing a long-barrelled 38 Special in a belt holster. "Can we talk in front of your nephew?"

Pip pleaded with his eyes.

"He's old enough to hear whatever you have to say."

"Fine. Look, by now you're probably figuring one of the stable hands tacked Brand for you this morning."

"A natural assumption."

"Matt, I don't want to scare you. But it wasn't any of them."

"Not to contradict but how do you know?" I indicated the vacant chair but he chose to pace.

"See.. I never told any of the hands which horse you would be riding. In fact I didn't even know what time you would get up." He looked out the window, leaning against the frame. "Figured you would just walk in there when you got ready and tell them yourself."

"Then what was Brand doing in the cross ties? And wearing the other horse's tack?"

"Someone's trying to *kill* your ass, Matt. That's all I can figure."

I glanced at Pip who looked frightened again. So I was careful to keep my tone analytical.

"How was he able to do his dirty work unseen?"

"The barn was empty." Dick ran his fingers through his white hair. "Pancho told me he was pitching hay on the other side of the yard for a good hour before he saw you. And the hand who was supposed to be on duty, Miguel, came in late because he had to drive his wife to her sister's funeral. So there was no one there to see what happened."

"Then it was only by the merest chance that the barn was deserted this morning. Tell me, Dick. Suppose one of the grooms had walked in and caught someone saddling that horse, What would he have done?"

"If he saw a stranger, he would have held him at bay with a pitchfork and raised Holy Hell."

"And the intruder would probably have been arrested for attempted horse theft."

"Probably.—Why? What are you thinking?"

"A stupid chance to take. Which suggests that the person was no stranger from off the road."

"If Miguel had caught a house guest in there, he'd have told the man or woman in high-decibel Spanish, that Brand was dangerous and not to be ridden.

"Then the man or woman would have said, "Oops. Is that so? I'll take another one then." And nobody would have suspected a sinister motive."

"Makes sense."

"So our anonymous groom must have had a right to be there."

"You mean whoever pulled the switch was one of us."

"More specifically one who heard your tale about Brand last night. Who also knew that I expected to ride a chestnut.—I'd eliminate you, Dick."

"Thanks."

"Because if you'd wanted to kill me, you wouldn't have sacrificed such a well-bred animal."

"You're right." Dick came to sit down at last and stretched out his legs. "I would have blown your head off with a shotgun and claimed I'd slipped in the mud. If I'd had a motive which I don't."

"We can also rule out Kim Berber as a suspect. I don't think she's tall enough or strong enough to get a saddle on a horse, even if she knew how."

"Which she wouldn't."

Pip was looking from one to the other of us as at a tennis match. "Should I write all this down?"

"Not necessary, dear Watson," I said.

Dick studied his boots of hippopotamus hide. "And you can't consider Farley either. I found out he's scared of horses."

"Scared of *getting on* them. Kim said he once took a bad spill during a cross-country ride. Which makes him a suspect like any other."

"How do you figure?"

"If Farley used to ride then he wouldn't have forgotten how to lead a horse out of a stall and get a saddle and bridle on it."

"But why would he want to put you on a runaway stallion? Are you vital to your cousin's campaign?"

"Don't flatter me. No, Farley hasn't the slightest reason to do me in. Moses Jones used to be a groom, so he too would have the means. But again not the motive."

"And that 'Son of Ham' wouldn't go stomping around in any barn where he might lose the shine off his precious shoes."

He unholstered his pistol. "Here, take this."

"Thanks, but I'd rather not be armed right now."

"You're ol' man bad luck this week, Matt. Your girl friend gets herself poisoned. Your cousin gets himself arrested for murder. And to top it off, you almost get your own ass sent to Hell. Seems to me you need a lot of protection. At least carry it while you're here."

"Pip and I are packing up to leave now. We'll be safe during the drive home, anyhow."

"Let's hope." Dick reholstered his gun, pulled in his long legs and stood up. "Hey you were crazy not to bail out. But thanks for saving the horse." He bent and shook my hand. "Voitier has got ten thousand from me and ten from my wife."

"Thank you."

"It's a lot less than the eventual worth of that stallion."

"When the door closed behind him, Pip jumped up and slapped my back. "Nice play, Shakespeare! If someone tried to kill you just to sabotage Armand's campaign, he had the opposite effect."

"I still don't accept that as a logical motive."

"What then?"

"Maybe we'll never know."

CHAPTER TWENTY-TWO
Saturday Afternoon

At Armand's Gentilly headquarters, a volunteer staff of six women and a youth, fortified with tepid coffee in styrofoam cups, stuffed envelopes while discussing the vital issues of the day: Glasnost, the Supreme Court vacancy, and Cher's nose.

A light-skinned woman with golden eyes waved a flier.

"'And the hunter is home from the hill'. They're in the back, Matt."

Armand was at a typewriter in his shirt sleeves, touch typing at awesome speed.

Ed Stokes, manning an old fashioned adding machine, hadn't yet relinquished his suit jacket. "Any news from Texas, Matt?"

"Two newses. The good news is that Dickerson is supporting Armand and he sent along this check." I held it in front of my cousin's face.

"Twenty thousand." He verified the amount then handed the check over to Edward. "What's the bad?"

"He still wanted to cover his bet with the other two. Gave Moses and Farley five thousand each."

"Rats!"

"It won't make much difference to Moses but it could buy Farley enough TV time to get back in the game."

"Farley's already back in," Ed sighed. "While he was away in Texas, a very nice surprise was delivered to his headquarters."

"A naked cow?"

"Even nicer than that," Armand said. "It was a certified check for one hundred grand. Enough to buy him spots on every channel."

"Who wants to see him that much?"

Ed pulled out a paper strip of figures. "Should I tell him, Armand? Right. Most of it came from the civic-minded workers of the Delta Purse factory. Every one of them gave a thousand bucks. What do you think of that?"

"Unbelievable is what I think. Without digging too far, you could learn that each of those loyal contributers had shortly before received a bonus of, maybe, eleven hundred."

"Probably. But more interesting is the fact that the Delta purse factory is owned by a company that is owned by another company which in turn is owned by.." He waited as though for a fanfare. "None other than Nat Ortigue."

"He's backing Moses."

"But spreading the sunshine around now. Ortigue and his wife each contributed ten thousand to Berber."

"I get it. New Orleans politics as usual."

Armand was stronger among the white voters. So Ortigue attempted to siphon off his racist vote by diverting it to an even whiter man on the other side. With the white vote split in half, Jones could possibly win by a clear majority in the first primary dispensing with the bother of a run-off. Ortigue's best investment could be contributions to Berber's campaign.

Armand said, "Don't forget the paddleboat event, Matt."

"I bought tickets. Don't tell me I'm expected to go."

"You sure are. You'll be representing my candidacy."

"Matt?" It was Dennis Quinn at my office door, the peach colored patches of covermark seemed larger under the bright office lights.

Steve was escorting him, looking grave as one does when walking very slowly to accommodate the feeble.

I rose and programmed a smile.

"Hello, Dennis. Sit down and let me get you something to drink."

"Tomato juice?" He waved Steve away and seated himself on the Fauteuil. "I have trouble keeping anything down."

Steve helped him off with his coat and the famous issue of

Spin could be seen poking out the inside pocket. Dennis waved at it. "Been showing that around. Everyone says it looks pretty good."

Steve stood uneasily with his back to the wall and sidled toward the door. He might have been in the presence of the scythe-wielding grim reaper himself. Finally he gave a half-bow and backed out of the office.

I already had some tomato juice spiced up to go in Bloody Marys but figured the hot sauce couldn't hurt him. I poured a tall glass-full and squeezed a lemon wedge on the brim. He took it in both hands and risked one tentative swallow.

I watched him, fearful for the Pakistani carpet. "What can I do for you?"

His long sigh seemed to cost him all his breath.

"Got to sell something else, Matt."

"Very well. What do you have for me?"

"You said you might want that secretary in the diningroom. What's it worth to you."

"I'll come over and give you an estimate."

He looked down at his hands then quickly looked up again.

"You'll pick it up when I move?"

"That's the agreement," I assured. "Not till you move."

After several more excrutiating minutes of forced cheerfulness, I called Steve to put Dennis in a cab then shut my office door. I looked up Didi's number and played its seven note tune on the phone. She answered with a languid, "Peek-a-boo-oo."

"Didi? This is Matt."

"Ooh! Ooh, Matt?" There was a delay while she (undoubtedly) called Robin to tip-toe over and put his big ear on the receiver. "Well Hi! How are you?"

"Lousy. I'm sending over some papers for you to pass on to Robin. Wherever he is."

"Oh.. Well.." (Buzz..buzz) "We.. I mean *I'll* wait for them. Anything else?"

"Yes. Tell Robin.. No, there's nothing else." I hung up without saying good-bye.

Steve looked in. "Matt? It's five-thirty. We're closing up

now."

"Good enough." I tossed him the envelope. "Have Gary drop this by Didi's on his way home."

"Maybe you'll want to wait on that?"

"Why?"

"Don't make amends for infidelity till it's over. The 'other woman' is right outside. Raymond Harris."

"Ask him in." Steve stood still a moment, smirking. "Good night and lock the door behind you. —And those papers to Didi's on the double."

"Like you say, chief." He saluted.

Raymond walked in shyly and sat as before with his brief case across his knees.

I said, "How are things in the enemy camp?"

"Search me." He shrugged. "I'm no longer aligned with the enemy, Matt."

"Oh? That's good news."

"My ambition has always been to make clients look as good as I possibly can. But then what you said after the debate the other night made me think. What if I actually helped put a homophobe into City Hall?"

"And subsequently got entrapped and arrested for sodomy."

"Or if anyone else did. No. I needed the job but it's not worth it."

"I know the Berber campaign is going to miss you. Now that they've lost Lloyd, your contribution is more important than before."

"That's what Farley said. He offered me more money." Raymond chuckled. "But I told him to let some God-fearing family man do his hair and make-up."

I laughed with him.

"The bad part is that since my work is finished, I'll be flying back to Chicago tonight."

"I'm sorry." I took his hand. "It was a great pleasure to know you."

He smiled shyly, "I hope it was." then unlocked the latch on his briefcase. "I stopped by here first because I want to help you find Rodger's murderer. Not that I cared about him, you understand. But I don't think the wrong person should be punished for it."

"George Sinclair is definitely the wrong person. But I have other names on my list."

He withdrew a manilla envelope and peered into it. "If Rodger had been killed in Chicago, your list would be three blocks long."

"I hadn't considered his historical enemies."

"It was sort of inevitable considering the way he did business. That's why I brought some data for you. —My late boss had some dirty tricks up his sleeve." Raymond waggled his Cross pen. "I wasn't in on all of his maneuvers but he used to brag that he provided full service to clients."

"What kind of service?"

"Besides making our man look good, he would do his best to make the opponent look bad. That was his tactic." He referred to one of those composition books with the splotchy black and white covers. My second grade teacher, Sister Margaret, used to show one like it to illustrate venial sin.

I asked, "How far would he go with that?"

"All the way. Rodger used to send an agent back to the man's home town and pore over newspaper and police records. Interview high school mates, army buddies…"

"Farley Berber asked him to do all that?"

"No. But then he didn't even know what was going on. The dragon lady ran the show."

"I heard Lloyd was Kim's idea."

"And she was his. The two of them were going at it like lovelorn alley cats up in Chicago. And I'm sure they strained a few springs in his hotel room here." He shrugged. "But that's irrelevant."

"Maybe not. Suppose Lloyd dug all around and didn't find any scandal?"

"In a kindergarten maybe." Raymond scoffed. "Every grown person has some bit of foolishness or indiscretion that can be twisted and exaggerated into a major case. A man smokes a joint at a frat party or cheats on a high school science quiz and it shows up in headlines twenty years later."

"When he's under the moral microscope."

He tapped the composition book. "This was especially effective during a three-way primary."

"How so?"

"Lloyd would get the two opponents each to rattle the other's skeleton while our client stepped back and decried the mud-slinging."

"Good strategy if he could work it."

"Easier than you think." He handed me the note book and I opened it to the first page: "New Orleans—Mayor"

"Did your boss find some skeletons here?"

"Pretty good ones because they haven't been rattled before. For example, he found Moses Jones listed with Orleans Parish Support Enforcement files."

"For what?"

"Back in seventy-two, a sixteen-year-old girl applied for welfare and named Jones as the father of her child. He has never acknowledged or supported the child to this day."

"Some other Moses Jones."

"No. She made a complete identification. She met him when he was working as a legal aid lawyer on behalf of abused children. How do you like that?"

"Completely out of character. Moses was happily married in '72 and a dedicated pro bono lawyer."

"I know." The young man smiled slyly. "This was especially juicy because Jones is big on that Jesse Jackson number of preaching family values and responsible fatherhood."

"I still don't believe it of Moses."

Raymond looked incredulous. "You're not hip, Matty. True or not, this accusation is in the case record. All we have to do is send a photocopy to the paper so Jones doesn't have enough time to refute it before the election."

"True or not, if it's a matter of record, no one can be sued. And if you get someone else to spill it, no mud gets on your man. Right?"

He smirked a smirk of yankee superiority. "New Orleans is such a backwater, I guess the science of dirty politics is new to you."

"You kidding? We study dirty politics in Sunday school around here. We have a special twist to that trick in Louisiana."

Raymond lit up. "Tell me. I love twists."

"When I want to win an election against, say, Huey Long, I just get my friend Jake to run in the same election. I pay his filing fees and expenses. Then Jake devotes all his TV spots to throwing mud at Huey Long and I stay clean."

"What if Jake encroaches on *your* vote."

"Easy. A week before the election, Jake drops out of the race with an impassioned speech about Huey Long's dirty tactics causing stress to his family."

"Mean, rotten, and underhanded. They'll love it in Chicago."

"Now I'll have to ask something I'd rather not know. Does my cousin have any skeletons?"

"Just one Matty, but it's a big, scary one. Rodger found out that Armand Voitier had passed for white back in college."

"Impossible! He's not that fair."

"You don't think so? He dated at least three white women and had a relationship with one while he was studying at USC in Berkeley."

"California? Now, I believe it. They hardly know the difference out there."

"It happened back in the sixties when everyone was into civil rights, too." Raymond said dispassionately. "So they didn't even care."

"In the deep south in the late 1980s they care very much." I made a fist and applied it smartly to the table. "Damn! Armand always had political ambitions. How could he have taken such a stupid chance?"

"Nothing terrible happened. I mean no marriage or mulatto babies ensued."

"It doesn't matter. If he even gave the appearance of denying his heritage, that would kill him dead with the black voters.

They already think he's too white for his own good."

"Rodger made the same point when he came up with this."

I looked somewhat hungrily at his composition book.

"What are you going to do with it now?"

"Dirty tricks were Rodger's game, not mine." He closed and locked his briefcase but kept the notebook in his hand. "Walk me to the door, Matty?"

We crossed the dim display floor together and I pulled out my door key. "I'll give you a lift to the airport."

"No, my transportation has been arranged. But thank you for the thought." He put his head down and studied me through his thick lashes for a long moment. Then he held out the notebook. "What I'm going to do is turn this over to you. For 'old times' sake'."

I clasped my hands around the record. "Thank you, kitten. I hope I have 'old times' with you again some day."

"It's a small world. Especially the gay world."

He smiled and then I had an irresistible urge. It was dark out and Royal Street was nearly deserted but still this was a foolish thing to do. I didn't weigh the consequences but just took him into my arms and kissed him hard.

My mind didn't become completely clear until after the single bullet smashed through the leaded glass door and hit him in the right temple, blowing away the left side of his head.

"Raymond?!"

I collapsed with him and he died in my arms before the expression could change on his face, so his eyes were still open.

I lay the boy on the floor as gently as though he were still alive then unlocked the door and yanked it open, another foolish act. Because the gunman may still have been out there and taking aim again.

In the alley across the street? On the third-floor balcony? I stood, a full-length target, and looked for him. But there was no sound or movement. And no second shot.

The street was very still as a city street gets after an episode of violence. Everyone but Matt Sinclair stays indoors and prays for whatever it is to go away. Or for it not to have meant anything.

I called 911 first, then Frank Washington's private number. He arrived twenty minutes after the Vieux Carré unit and the door was open for him. Frank barrelled into the shop, suit jacket flapping and gasped when he saw Raymond's body.

"My God, it's Robin! You didn't say!"

"No, Frank. This man's name is Raymond Harris. But thank you for coming so fast."

He looked more closely then stopped and put his hand over his heart. "Oh. Say, you have blood on your coat. You must have been close when the shot was fired."

A patrolman came through the door holding up a shell in a glassine bag.

"We know it came from directly across the street. The gun man didn't stop to pick up his casing." He handed Frank a clip board with the preliminary report.

"He didn't stop for anything," I offered. "He'd disappeared by the time I unlocked the door and got out there."

Frank perused the report. "You'd already closed for the night?"

"Yes. Raymond and I were alone here."

"Just you and the victim, Raymond Harris, hmm? He was a friend?"

"He was only in town a few days, we…Yes. A friend."

"Welcome to New Orleans." He stepped outside, made a quick survey of the street, then came back and examined the door, putting a finger through the nickle-sized hole in the pane.

"Man had damned good eyesight. To hit his mark dead-on through a door of leaded glass into an unlighted store on a dark street."

"He could see Raymond's blond hair through the window," I said. "The kid was an easy target."

Two of the coroner's men covered the aluminum stretcher, hoisted on three, and carried Raymond away. He was light. Easy to lift.

We Sinclairs never show much emotion, but I must have

looked agitated. Frank gripped my shoulder.

"I'm sorry, Matt. I know this must be hard on you."

"No, not me. Don't worry about me."

"At least we're keeping your name out of it for now. But by tomorrow all the newspeople will know it's your shop and that you were the only witness."

"That doesn't matter now."

"Then I'll need a few answers. Most murders have to be solved within twenty-four hours—"

"Or they never get solved. I know."

"Then try to give me a clue. What brought the victim to New Orleans?"

"Raymond came down from Chicago to work on Farley Berber's TV spots. His employer was the late Rodger Lloyd."

"That murder last week? So there's a connection." Frank uncapped his Bic. "Two colleagues from Chicago, killed by unknown assailants nine days and two blocks apart. The M.O.s were different. But I don't believe in coincidences." He wrote "See Rodger Lloyd" in the margin of the Original Offense Report. "The answer may be up north somewhere. Unless you know of someone who had a motive here in town."

"Absolutely nobody. He didn't even know anyone except the Berber campaign people and me."

"I wouldn't look too hard at the Berber faction. They should have *loved* him for the job he did on those commercials. And as for you.."

"I should have loved him too."

"I guessed that's how it was." He didn't make a notation of that salient fact and let me see he wasn't making one. "Matt, I don't want to bring this up. But Robin might have had a motive."

"What?!"

He waved his hands in a conciliatory motion. "I know he's not capable of murder. But it might just occur to somebody else. And there's another angle you'd better consider. Suppose the gunman wasn't after Harris at all?"

"Well then.." I stopped and realized what he was driving at.

"Me?! You think he was aiming at *me*?"

"By your own observation, nobody in town knew Raymond Harris. Everyone knows Matt Sinclair."

"I wasn't the intended, Frank. I ran outside right afterward and stood there on the sidewalk. If he'd wanted me he'd have spent another thirteen cents."

"Assuming he hadn't panicked and run after the first shot." Frank looked me up and down. "We're almost through here. – I suggest you run that cashmere jacket right over to Moon's Dry Cleaners. Those protein stains are the devil to get out."

CHAPTER TWENTY-THREE
Saturday Evening

When I got home to Esplanade Ave., the lights were on, the dulcet tones of Luther Van Dross filled the house and something was cooking and sending steam and spicy aromas from the kitchen.

On hearing the front door close, Robin came skipping into my arms. "Oh Matty! I got the papers an hour ago. A home in my own name! Now I *know* you love me!"

My arms closed around him automatically. "Kitten.."

He bubbled on. "I stopped for some crawfish and I'm fixing you jambalaya and a hot Cajun potato salad." At last he felt my stiffness. "But what's wrong? This should be the best night of our relationship!"

"Something happened…"

"Wha –?" He pulled back. "Matty, is this blood on your sleeve?"

"Raymond Harris's. He was shot and killed this evening."

"Raymond?" Robin stood away. "Wasn't he the one..?"

"Yes. On his way back to Chicago tonight. And he was just telling me goodbye when it happened. By the door." No need to say we were kissing. "They have no idea who did it."

"Oh, I'm *sorry* Matt."

"Me too." I took off my bloody coat and handed it to him. "I hope you don't mind that I can't eat."

"No, I understand. I'll just put everything in freezer bags. They have these blue and yellow lines that turn green when you close them."

"Good."

I would have cried for young Raymond Harris but Sinclairs

don't cry. So I just spent the rest of the evening in the living room with the phone turned off and a book I wasn't reading. Robin had sense enough to stay in the back and leave me to my dark reverie. The bedroom phone rang several times and he answered it and gracefully deflected the callers' invitations to assorted fêtes and soirées.

At ten-fifteen the phone rang for the last time, and Robin thought this call worth disturbing me for. He tip-toed into the living room, looked carefully to assure that I wasn't asleep or dead and whispered. "It's Sylvia."

"I'd better take it." I turned on the phone in front of me and picked it up.

"Hello, Sylvia."

"Matt? We're all upset here. We just heard on the news that a man was murdered in your store."

"His name was Raymond."

"Philip almost collapsed when it came on. He was so frightened. Wait, I'll give him the phone."

"Uncle?" My nephew's voice could always raise my spirits even in this kind of time. "I almost had a heart attack. It could have been *you* they killed!"

"No, I don't think they were aiming at me."

"Please take care of yourself."

Robin tactfully left me alone in my bed but even so I didn't sleep till after I'd heard the clock chime five times.

CHAPTER TWENTY-FOUR
Sunday Morning

I never set an alarm but I usually awake naturally around seven-thirty. The day after Raymond's murder I didn't make it into the dining room till nearly ten.

Robin was sitting at the table with the *Times-Picayune* propped against a candle stick. He snapped to attention. "Eggs for breakfast, Matty?"

"No. Nothing—Are you into the paper already?"

"Raymond Harris's picture is on page three. He was really cute."

"I don't want to see it."

"You're going to think I'm really awful for saying this."

I didn't want to wait for coffee so I took his in spite of the cream and sugar. "What?"

"I couldn't help wondering what if I had been with you in the store. The killer would have thought *I* was him and shot *me*."

"But he didn't."

"I shouldn't have worried about it then."

"No, you shouldn't have. Give me the second section. I want to see how the campaign is going."

Robin unfolded the paper. "Farley Berber has gained ten more points in the polls."

"You can keep it."

I was lining up my daily ration of vitamins when the kitchen phone shrilled. Robin went in to answer it then came back with his hand over the receiver and mouthed 'Frank Washington'."

"Hello Frank."

"Guess what? We have a suspect in last night's murder."

"Thank God! Who is it?"

"Your cousin George Sinclair."

"You're a lousy comedian, Frank. George is locked up."

"Not since two o'clock yesterday afternoon when the Teachers' Union put up his bail."

"Two o'clock?"

"He had plenty of time to shower and shave, take a walk, load his pistol and make it down to Royal Street by five-thirty."

"That's preposterous."

"Harris was killed with a thirty-eight. George Sinclair admits to owning a thirty-eight Target Master, but we couldn't do a ballistics because he seems to have misplaced it. And he has no alibi. Sorry, we took him back into custody an hour ago."

"My cousin had never even met Raymond Harris much less had a reason to kill him."

"That brings me to a frightening theory, Matt. Suppose George didn't want to kill young Harris at all. I think he was after you."

"Me? What for?"

"What for? Money! Wake up to reality. How much are you worth in your own right?"

"I'm comfortable."

"Close to a million, I'd guess."

"Nowhere near."

"And it's no secret that George is your closest Sinclair relative. A man will kill for less."

"Taking a viewpoint every bit as cynical as your own, I would have to say your theory is horse apples."

"I'm listening."

"Sinclairs have eagle eyes and rock-steady hands. And any one of us can geld a gnat at two hundred yards."

"Meaning you're a gun-happy tribe."

"Meaning if George had wanted to kill me, I'd be dead."

The second I hung up, Robin leaned over me and straightened my tie. "Why don't you take your mind off all this, Matty. Let's drive out to the Lakeside mall and look for draperies."

"We already have draperies."

He flapped his hand. "Oh, those were okay for *your* house. But this is *our* house now."

"Which doesn't change the basic structure of the building."

"Oh, I'm bubbling with inspiration. What do you think of fuchsia satin for the bathroom?"

"I think I've created a decorator's nightmare. In any case, I have more vital matters on my mind." I turned the last page of Raymond's composition book. I had memorized every entry. "A man was murdered last night and this may hold the motive."

"Would that motive be good for Rodger Lloyd too?"

"It would."

"What about Karen?"

"I don't see how." I slipped the book into my briefcase. "Karen is no more than an enthusiastic political supporter."

"If she's not that important to anybody, why did someone poison her?"

"That's what I have to find out. I'm going back to see the candidates today."

"They won't be working on a Sunday."

"The Sunday before the election they'll be working like maniacs." I stood up. "I'll call the boys to come with me. They could use an outing."

CHAPTER TWENTY-FIVE
Sunday Morning

Pip parked us on the neutral ground of North Claiborne under the I-Ten Overpass.

"This isn't such a good neighborhood," Ronald allowed.

"That's why I brought my two brave nephews along." I picked up my briefcase and opened the door. "Stay with the car."

Moses Jones's store front headquarters was still over-run with hungry-looking women and children. When I walked in, Moses was chatting with some of his constituents while carrying a giggling little girl on his shoulders, bobbing up and down to give her a proper ride.

The child wore thread-bare hand–me-downs but was scrubbed and groomed within an inch of her life with three plaits, painstakingly combed and ribboned.

"Matt Sinclair!" Moses shifted the child to his left hip and shook my hand. "We were just talking about that murdered man. What was his name? The paper said he worked for Rodger Lloyd."

"Raymond Harris. He was also my friend."

"Oh.. Oh." He looked embarrassed for a second then put the child down, carefully standing her on her feet. "Jawanda? You go back over there and help your Mama." Jawanda toddled off on her mission and Moses drew me into his unpopulated back office.

"Terrible thing to happen to those men. Totally senseless."

"The murders made sense to somebody. Probably the same motive in both cases."

"But why?" His eyes narrowed. "Does this have something to do with the primary?"

"I've been thinking about that." I dug into my brief case. "All Raymond had in common with his late employer was some nasty information about the candidates."

Now alerted, Moses placed hands on hips and leaned backward, tilting his chin up. "Give."

"On Moses Jones... Excuse me." I paged through Raymond's composition book and found the relevant entry. "In 1972, a minor named Della Watkins told Support Enforcement that you were..."

He interrupted me with a palm-out "stop" sign.

"I know! I know how it goes. I'm supposed to be the father of that girl's child."

"Are you?" I turned to lay the book on his desk and picked up a wooden ruler. "I thought not." I placed the ruler along the inside spine of the note book and carefully tore out the pertinent pages while he paced the floor.

"That girl was being sexually abused by her own father. Her natural father! I was speaking for her as a court-appointed guardian because no one in the family would testify." He inveighed at the ceiling. "Naturally! And all the neighbors were afraid, so it was just me and that child against the system. Then right in the middle of it all, the poor girl.—Her name was Della?—Yes. Della had a baby. You *know* she wouldn't name her own father. And when he ordered her to accuse me, she had no choice."

I handed him the pages. "Has the record ever been cleared?"

He took them without seeming to notice what they were.

"Not officially. I mean my denial is in the case record. If you tracked down that girl, I'm sure she would tell the truth now."

"Unless she had a reason not to."

"She wouldn't be scared of her old man anymore. He got himself killed in a knife fight a few years back."

"Suppose someone paid her not to exonerate you."

"I don't share your cynicism. My constituents know me."

"But not Support Enforcement. I'd publicize the whole truth if I were you."

"How's that?"

"Before someone comes out with the *half*-truth." The "ven-ial sin" book went back into my briefcase. It had one more appearance to make this afternoon.

"Yeah." Now Moses scanned the pages in his hand. "Yeah, I know what you mean. Thank you, Matt."

"That's not the worst news. Someone may think that item constitutes a motive."

"For what?"

"Murder. Rodger Lloyd and Raymond Harris both had the information that would damage your campaign. And they both died of unnatural causes."

The candidate turned a darker shade of black. "Matt, you don't think *I* could have killed those two men!"

"Not you. But suppose someone else did on your behalf and without your knowledge."

"Just who do you mean?"

"Your most passionate supporter. Nathan Ortigue."

"Not a chance."

"Ortigue wants you in the Mayor's office very badly. And he's got plenty of thugs on the payroll to assure that he gets any-thing he wants. All he has to do is point and grunt."

"I'll concede the man has an attitude." Moses rolled up the damning pages and wrung them like a chicken's neck. "But killing in cold blood isn't his style."

"Who says?" I locked my briefcase. "You don't know who you're playing with here. Nat Ortigue got where he is by using muscle."

"I know his reputation."

"And if he never actually killed anyone, that's only because no one has ever been brave enough to get in his way."

"Hey, these are the facts of life, dig?" Moses strode to the office door and looked out on the sandwich and doughnut line. "You see Florence Leonard over there in the pink sweater? Her six-year-old, Tevis, is hopelessly retarded." He whirled back around. "The boy was born *normal*, Matt. You know how he got brain-damaged?"

"No.. I don't."

"Chewing lead-based paint off the window sills in the St Thomas Project. *That's* how!"

"I'm sorry."

"Babies chew paint, right?" He made a fist and punched the air. "So hundreds of those project kids are growing up retarded and no one gives a shit. It's the city government's business to make those buildings safe for our children. But no New Orleans Mayor, black or white, has considered them worth his time. Those people out there are the powerless ones. They *need* a Moses Jones in City Hall." He closed the door and came back to the desk. "And at this point, *I* need a big time power broker to get me into a position where I can help them."

"Not that one."

"Listen to me, Matt. Once I'm in office, I know I can handle Nat Ortigue."

"You don't have a spoon long enough."

Pip drove us onto I-Ten for the shortest route from Moses Jones's inner city headquarters to Farley Berber's Rodeo Emporium out on Airline Highway.

I left my nephews browsing through the racks of western wear while I walked back to the office whose door was still propped open. "Hello, Farley. Do you have a moment?"

The candidate was still wearing his "man of action" clothes from L.L. Bean. Raymond had probably buried the cowboy suits.

"Sure thing, Matt." He didn't leave his desk but just bobbed up and held his hand out in greeting. The sleeves of his plaid flannel lumberjack shirt were pushed up to expose the forearms of an old man, their flesh a hairless yellow parchment. He waved at the bar. "Just take you a drink. I expect you need it after what happened to that poor young fella. Right in your shop, I heard."

"Raymond was a friend."

"That so? Didn't know you were close." He rolled his chair back. "Harris was a good man. Knew his business."

"You must have been put off when he quit your campaign."

"Sure as shootin'. But he made the good effort while he was here, and I'm sincerely sorry he got himself killed." He opened a box of cigars to me and I shook my head. "They have any notion who did it?"

"My notion is the same one who murdered Raymond's employer, Rodger Lloyd."

"News on the radio said they got that particular miscreant back in jail." Farley crossed his legs which didn't seem so lanky now in cordoroys.

"You heard wrong. My cousin George is innocent."

"Reckon that'll be up to twelve men good 'n' true."

"No, it will be up to me." The bar was fully stocked and featured a bottle of Wild Turkey for a smooth Sazerac. But I wouldn't be in his debt for a real drink so settled for half a glass of tomato juice. "I'll find the real murderer before it ever gets to court."

Berber tucked his chin in. "Even Perry Mason waits till the trial."

"Rodger Lloyd was a walking motive. When he worked for a campaign, he would hunker down and dig up all the hidden scandals of the rival candidates."

"That's dirty tricks and somethin' I'd never personally approve of."

"Reason enough for someone to kill him. Don't you think?"

"Maybe so." Berber's eyes shifted. "But as the man was on my side, he wouldn't have been digging after me."

"He wouldn't have to." I knocked back the tomato juice. "My cousin George was accused of acting from jealousy. His wife and the victim had been lovers back in the early seventies."

"Some men have long memories and short tempers."

"But if that was the motive, why not a more recent cuckold?" I placed my palms down on the desk blotter and leaned over him. "Like you, yourself."

Farley's thin shoulders stiffened. "What are you inferrin'?"

"You're inferring. I'm implying. That your wife Kim and

Rodger Lloyd were lovers."

He looked away from me and shrugged weakly. "Every woman needs a hobby. Mine don't care for bridge."

"You condoned the affair then?"

"I didn't tuck 'em in, but I had no problem with it." He turned his chair around on its casters and looked out the window.

"I'm an old man, Matt. In some ways even older than that. My wife is a very beautiful woman. I can't live without her so I make concessions. Simple as that."

He didn't turn around again and I left him there, staring out the window into an asphalt alley. He'd made his bargain and would keep it.

Out in the lot, my nephews were playing the car radio. Some abominible top forty station was playing "La Bamba". The new Los Lobos version because Richie Valens is dead too.

Ronald climbed into the back seat and Pip took the wheel.

"Did you learn anything, uncle?"

"Farley Berber is innocent."

"So is my father."

"I know, and we'll find the real murderer. But not here at the Rodeo Emporium."

At Armand Voitier's Headquarters, a quadroon in Williwear was watching a video tape of Thursday night's debate and shaking her head. "Buzz words, that's what we need. What do you think, Matt?"

"Okay, 'leadership', 'government waste', 'moral values', 'emphasis on education', 'high-level corruption'... Put them in any order you want."

"Tell that to the guys. They're back there writing tonight's speech."

In the back room, Ed Stokes was sorting through the chaff of past speeches trying to glean an oratorical grain of wheat. "How about this? 'We'll return the Port of New Orleans to its former predominance as the second busiest in the country!'"

"Good." Armand conveyed this to the typewriter. "Now tell me how?"

"I.. " Ed scanned the speech fruitlessly. "Okay, you'll commission a study on the issue, compiled by experts."

"What experts?" Armand looked up from his keyboard and spied me. "Hello Matt. Take a look at Farley's new campaign flier." He handed it across to me.

This was like the previous one but featured two photographs instead of three. Berber's picture on the right (naturally) stalwartly faced down a flattering likeness of Moses Jones on the left. The text stressed the Republican's stand in favor of motherhood and the American flag without throwing any sharp stones at his liberal opponent.

I made an airplane out of it. "If they spread enough of these around, they may get the voters thinking it's a two-man race."

"And remember that Moses is doing the same on his end. Every speech he's made has been directed against 'my honorable opponent, Mr. Berber,'" Armand frowned. "They've ganged up on us, but we'll have to deal with them separately."

Edward caught my airplane. "How do you figure?"

"We've got two opponents. But remember, we only have to beat *one* of them this time around." My cousin took a swig of warm, flat cola. "We'll operate like a wolf pack. Decide which of our opposition is weaker and try to cut into his vote."

The *Times-Picyune* was curled up in the waste basket and I fished it out. "This morning's poll says Farley is gaining while Moses is staying about the same. So he looks more vulnerable."

"Also, blacks don't vote in the same proportion as whites." Edward affixed a paper clip to the nose of the airplane and shot it back to me.

Armand nodded over his decision. "We'll write off Farley's constituency and go after Moses then."

"Check." Edward picked up a yellow pad. "Where does that strategy take us? Should we buy spots on the black radio stations?"

"Waste of money." Armand snapped. "Moses has blanketed that medium so thoroughly people would probably think its just another ad for him."

Edward made a note and underlined it. "How about making a personal appearance in the projects?"

"No good. Not only are we all liable to get mugged, but the people would resent the gesture at this late date. 'Who he think *he* be, that white nigger?"

"The projects are solid for Moses," I agreed. "But the working poor can still be had. They resent the welfare class and get more conservative by the hour."

Armand took the paper from me and made a face.

"Look at that whopping undecided vote. All those voters are going to stay home on Election Day unless we give them a reason to come out. I hope you'll give them a few on the paddle-boat."

"I'll try to be eloquent."

"Say, Matt." Armand took his glasses off. "I want to tell you, we're very sorry about young Harris."

"I'm going to try to make it up to him. By finding his murderer."

"Do you figure it was linked with the Lloyd case?"

"I think they were both killed by the same man. Possibly for what they knew."

Armand went back to his speech, rolling up the sheet of paper for an edit. "What could they have known?"

"We don't care what they knew about the others. All that concerns us is what they knew about you."

"What's that?" He asked it lightly in the tone of an innocent man.

"That you passed for white back in college."

"I...? Oh, Lord!" He put his elbows on the desk and covered his face with both hands. "That was the year I spent at Berkley. Hey, those were crazy times."

I took out my composition book and flipped to the Voitier chapter. "Unfortunately, these times aren't crazy. They're merely vicious."

"I know.. I know." He spoke from behind his hands. "Try to understand, Matt. When I first arrived in Southern California I experienced this tremendous culture shock. I saw

this 'Brave New World' out there with no prejudice, no segre-
gated lunch counters. White dorms..colored dorms.." He let
the hands drop but wouldn't meet my eyes. "I know what it
looks like now. But back then it didn't seem wrong."

"Passing for white?"

"I swear I never told anyone I was white." Armand took a
long breath and let it out. "I just never said I wasn't."

"And those California hippies didn't know the difference."

"Hell, everyone had a tan. I didn't look or sound any different. And nobody treated me any different. So after a while I
didn't feel any different."

"All that could be explained. But not that you slept with a
white woman."

"They know that too?" He shook his head. "Worse than
white, she was *blond*. Kirsten Norgaard. She was an
Anthropology major, brilliant, passionate, and beautiful like
no other girl." He closed his eyes, perhaps recalling her face.
"One night in the Spring term, we were all having one of those
philosophical conversations around a candle stuck in a Chianti
bottle. You remember those?"

"It was my generation too," I said. "Incense, pot, and cheap
wine."

"Right. We had Day-Glow posters by Peter Max on the
walls. These beaded curtains..."

"Strobe lights, granny glasses, and The Incredible String
Band."

"You've got the picture, Matt. We were all children in the
'Family Of Man'.—You want some coffee? No?" He rose and
walked around his office in the bright light of florescence and
1987. "Well, one night I was just lying there on the crash pad
with my head in Kirsten's lap..." He went to the coffee maker
and poured himself a precise cup to the brim, spilling none.

"So I was sipping Bali Hai out of a wine skin and a whole
bunch of us were having this relevant discussion about Selma
and Bull Conners and the sticks and the hoses." He sipped the
coffee and frowned. "I said I wished I'd been marching with
Doctor King and how some of my ancestors were slaves. Then

you know what Kirsten said?"

"I know what any Southern woman would have said."

There were scissors on the desk so I busied myself cutting outy the damning pages.

"But all that girl said was, 'Hey gang! Army has negro blood. Isn't that groovy'? As though 'having negro blood' didn't make me black. What do you think of that?"

"Groovy."

"I even believed it myself. That was 'The Age of Aquarius'. 'The times they were a-changing'. Remember?"

"So we believed. But they never changed that much, Armand."

"Oh, I well understood that when I finally came home to New Orleans in the Spring. I decompressed the minute I climbed off that Trailways Bus." He put the coffee down because it didn't taste like Bali Hai. "Right there in the station were those two drinking fountains side by side. 'White' and 'Colored'. Welcome home to reality, Sambo. The 'Age of Aquarius' is over."

"I'm sorry, cousin."

He sighed and shook his head minutely. "So I resumed my rightful place in society, enrolled at Tulane Law School, dated Autocrat daughters… I wrote one last letter to Kirsten saying I had fallen in love with another girl." He smiled thinly. "And then just a few years later, sure enough I did."

"Claudia is a beautiful woman."

"And my kind." He met my eyes steadily, having completed the trip of two decades forward to the present. "Ultimately I'm glad the way it turned out. You see, if I'd married Kirsten, I'd have had to stay out there in California and turn white. It would have been like amputating my history."

"If that nasty piece of your history ever gets out, the white men of the region will want to lynch you."

He shook his head. "There won't be anything left to hang up by the time the black women are finished with me.

CHAPTER TWENTY-SIX

Sunday Afternoon

Ronald popped into the back seat. "This has been a very political day, Uncle. You've interviewed all three candidates. Do you think one of them killed Mr. Lloyd?"

"They all had better motives than your father. Beyond that, I've made no conclusion."

Pip started the ignition. "Now for the best part. We're going to the Sinclair mansion."

"More accurately, The St. Bernadette Nursing Home."

A young nun opened the front door to us, but the Mother Superior, Sister Jeremy herself, was in the drawing room to receive the visitors.

"So glad you could come, Matt." She wasn't trendy enough to go into "civies", but wore a modern habit in navy with mid-calf length skirt and a short veil over her graying hair. "And who are these handsome young men?"

"Allow me to present my nephews, Sister: Philip and Ronald. Two more Sinclairs."

But one wasn't. That I didn't say.

"And fine boys they are." She addressed them with no condescension. "Matthew comes on 'Open House Day' every year to check the property."

"Naturally, I don't trust you for a second, Sister. You might have turned this house into a bowling alley or a casino since my last tour."

Sister Jeremy stepped back. "Why, Matthew, of course we did. But we've carefully covered the alleys with rugs and hidden the wheels out in the shed. So you won't catch us this year either."

A fresh party of visitors claimed her attention and she had to excuse herself. "Please try some of our tea and cakes. And then you're free to wander at will, except for the occupied guest rooms."

Pip ignored the refreshment table. He was gazing through the front hall and up the staircase at the balcony.

"Uncle Matt, that's so grand. Like in an old movie."

"I remember how I used to huddle up there in my Doctor Dentons, peeking through the railing at mother's parties." If I squinted, I could almost see my three-year-old self doing that. "Come on. I'll show you the upstairs."

Pip moved so fast that he hit the landing ten steps ahead of me while Ronald trailed behind.

On reaching the second floor, I assumed my accustomed role as guide. I had given this tour before.

"Of most historical interest are the Sinclair family protraits along the wall. They're still hung in chronological order."

I paused at the oil rendering at the head of the staircase. Even the most flattering protraitist couldn't depict comeliness in its gaunt subject with his pale hair, prominent nose, and receding chin.

"This painting of Juan Pedro San Claro was done in 1798. He was our first ancestor born in the new world."

"San Claro?" Ronald pushed his glasses up his nose. "I thought we were French. Why did he have a Spanish name?"

"Remember that New Orleans was under Spanish rule from 1760 to 1800. Everyone who wanted to get along swore allegiance to King Carlos of Spain and adopted the language."

Pip had been drawn to the next portrait, of a stunning brunette for any age. "Who was she? And can I go back in time and get fixed up with her?"

"Catherine Potin was the daughter of a French Captain garrisoned in Mobile. She became Juan Pedro's bride in the St. Louis Cathedral in 1775."

Ronald looked from one portrait to the other and back again.

"How did that yucky-looking guy rate such a doll?"

"It wasn't Juan Pedro's looks that won her. His father, Artur St. Clair, had amassed the largest fortune in the colony."

Pip was impressed. "An eighteenth-century Donald Trump? That's fantastic!"

Soon after emigrating from France, Artur became a money lender. He dispensed soft bills of credit from the Company Of India and got back hard livres. Gold."

"Doesn't sound very ethical," Ronald allowed.

"There was no Securities Exchange Commission in the colony. Anyway, Juan Pedro was considered the most eligible of bachelors despite his looks."

"He had it made," Pip breathed.

"Enough to capture the prettiest maiden in the territory. Our family means have waxed and waned over the generations. But Sinclairs who inherit money traditionally marry for beauty and charm."

Pip clapped his hands. "Good deal! So then the Sinclairs who've inherited beauty and charm can marry for money!"

"Such has been the custom."

He made his lips a thin line.

"I wish my father had followed the custom."

"Be proud of him, Pip. George is a fine man with a good sense of values. Money isn't all-important."

"Unless you don't have it."

I resumed my personal history lesson. "In 1800, Spain deeded the Louisiana territory back to France which kept it only three years. Then Napoleon sold us off to the Yanks." We had moved on to the next portrait of an ancestor less unsightly. "Juan Pedro's son, Matteo San Claro, kept up with the times. He changed our name again, to Sinclair."

"Which it shall remain until the Russians take over," Ronald offered cynically.

Pip studied the face of his five-times' great-grandfather. "He looks a little like you, Uncle Matt."

"So I've been told before. Some traits keep recurring throughout the generations. Next is Matteo's son, John Sinclair, who was named after President Adams. He died young of the fever. And here is John's son Maximillian who owned the biggest plantation in the region. He had two wives. The second was black."

Ronald looked dubious. "I don't see *her* picture up here."

"Nor will you. We're descended from the white one."

I stopped at the largest and most elaborate in the row of portraits. Its subject was a tall, blond equestrian in formal riding garb, his crop dangled carelessly over his shoulder.

"This was painted in 1883. Ernest was my great-grandfather and your great-great." I turned on the lamp over the portrait. "He was Maximillian's youngest white son and the only one not to bear arms for the Confederacy. He spent the war years studying in France."

Pip assessed the costume, the rakish tilt of the hat and the insoucient expression on the lips. The Victorian artist's skill was such that they seemed to curl into a smirk even as we watched.

"He looks like a racy character. I wish I could have known him."

"No you don't. Ernest was a dangerous and violent maniac. The family lost almost everything betting on the South. But what little remained, that man squandered on drink, gambling, and women."

"Women?"

"Nothing to smile about. No one did more to bring disgrace on our name. Since that man, no Sinclair child has ever been named Ernest nor ever will be."

Ronald tilted his head and the light reflected from his glasses. "It appears we had a rotten apple in the family tree."

"We've had quite a few, but Ernest was the rottenest. He started out bad." I was eager as always to impart family gossip passed down through generations of aunties in kitchens. "Even as a child, he was a notorious bully and sadist, abusing younger children and helpless birds and animals. As he grew older, he learned to conceal his bent personality. So successfully that he was allowed into the best drawing rooms and permitted to court the gentlest maidens in the South."

"I'll bet he had them too," Ronald said flippantly. "He was just the kind girls seem to like."

"No doubt. He won the hand of Genevieve Stevens, a rich, beautiful, and impeccably-bred daughter of the Confederacy. But even in her charming company he grew more malevolent and more dangerous every year. He abused Genevieve and their children. He once kicked her down those very stairs, crippling her and killing the baby she was carrying. Modern psychiatry would call Ernest a Sociopath."

Pip seemed to flinch at the term.

"You mean your great-grandfather was insane?"

"Not by legal definition. The man knew right from wrong but simply didn't care. His long career of enormities culminated in the year 1910. He got into a fit of drunken rage and shot a black farmer dead up in St. Landry Parish."

Pip gazed up at the portrait as though trying to read the mind of its subject, long gone, buried, and forgotten by all but a few Sinclairs. "What for?"

"There didn't have to be a reason. Maybe the man didn't snatch his hat off fast enough or call him 'Monsieur'."

"Are you telling us our great-great grandfather was hanged for murder?"

"Not a chance. The case was continued for years to give all the witnesses time to forget or die. Then finally it was declared a matter of 'self-defense'. And Ernest went out and celebrated with a three-day binge in Shantytown."

"I'll bet he bought his way out of it," Pip said in wonderment.

"And not cheaply. By the time great-grandmother Genevieve finished paying off the judge, there was no money left in his family or in hers."

Ronald unconsciously shifted into a horse stance, balancing his weight precisely, and made two tight fists. He seemed more angry about this eighty-year-old crime than any more recent.

"Don't tell me he got completely away with it! Nothing happened to him?"

I had to decide whether they were old enough for the truth. Pip, anyway, looked like a man already.

"Something happened to him." I waited till both their eyes were on me. "Where Sinclairs have thought they were above the law, sometimes Sinclairs have had to *be* the law."

"How's that?"

I took a deep breath then said it. "Ernest's brother, my great-grand-uncle Louis, took him on a hunting trip. Ernest never returned."

Two pairs of large eyes, one pair blue, one brown were both horrified and impressed.

Ronald was the first to find his voice.

"Are you telling us it was an execution? Fratricide?"

"More like the extermination of a misgotten monster. Before he could hurt anyone else."

Pip said, "But how can a man shoot down his own brother?"

"It wasn't a job to be entrusted to outsiders. Sometimes we ourselves have to cull out the bad ones." I tapped his arm. "Let's skip down to the last portrait. The most recent master of this house was my father and your grand-uncle, Arthur Sinclair."

"He was quite handsome," Ronald said politely.

Pip was looking beyond. "There's still space there for *your* picture, Uncle."

"I haven't sat for one."

He stepped down to the end of the hall then and slapped the bare wall. "And right here will be mine!"

CHAPTER TWENTY-SEVEN

Sunday Afternoon

Back in the house on Banks Street, Sylvia's kitchen was dingier than ever now that George wasn't on the premises to exercise even his slight control. The châtelaine slumped at the table partaking of a Scooter Pie washed down with Pop Rouge.

"You sure you don't want any, Matt?"

"Honestly. Yes."

"Because it wouldn't be any trouble."

"I'm sure." I looked behind the curtain and the window box was gone, probably just relocated. I could detect faint traces of its harvest in the atmosphere.

She read my mind and waved the air guiltily. "Now what are you inviting us to tomorrow night?"

"It's a political fund-raiser. The Forum For Good Government chartered the *Julep Queen* for the night. There will be dinner, dancing to the orchestra... And then breakfast the next morning."

"Out on the river?"

"That's where they keep the boats. I bought four tickets expecting to distribute them among Steve and the staff."

Sylvia rested her elbows on a Star cover photo of Dolly Parton with its promise to reveal her diet secrets.

"And they turned down a chance to go?"

"They all declined for reasons of sickness, health or old age. So I thought you and the boys might enjoy the cruise."

"I don't know.." Her voice faltered. "I should be bummed out about poor George. But then he refused to let you spring him, so he's making his own Karma—You think there's anything I can do for him now?"

"Just keep your mouth shut. If the police learn that one of your sons is by Rodger Lloyd, it may be considered to strengthen his motive."

"Oh, that's a crock. If it were so important to George, he would have wanted to know which boy it was. Don't you think? And he never even asked. Now, what if they keep digging and make me tell?"

All of a sudden I didn't want her to tell. What if Philip were the bastard? Would I love him any less if he turned out not to be my blood?

"That's sort of settled then. About the boat, I mean. We'll go." She moved toward the door and as she opened it, we heard footsteps hurrying away.

I was alerted. "Is someone trying to get in?"

She shook her head. "Don't worry, that was just my son. He's into listening at doors, lately. I don't know why."

"In that case he's heard our conversation about him."

"No, not him. The other son."

Decatur Street faces the wharves and the river. Going toward Poland Avenue there are few residences and street lamps are scarce. It's no place to walk alone at night. But I hadn't wanted to leave my car unattended in that neighborhood so I arrived at Dennis Quinn's house *sur Baie et Bleu* as the Cajun's say; On shanks' mare.

Dennis's gingerbreaded Victorian had been constructed as a double but was later converted to a single residence by Dennis and his late companion Wendall. They had installed an authentic gas lamp at the front door above the mailbox but it wasn't lit though the sun was darkening to an indigo haze.

I stopped at the iron gate and rang the bell, then it was several minutes before Dennis appeared and tottered down the front steps to admit me. He didn't bother to wear the Covermark in his own home and the raspberry colored blotches were visible on his face and arms as he unlocked the gate.

"Evening, Matt." His breathing was shallow, his voice weak.

"Say, I could come back if this isn't a good time."

"No time is good anymore. Come on in." He preceded me up the front steps, taking them cautiously and I stopped behind him as he negotiated each one, feeling with his toe first then sliding his foot across the creaking wooden boards and shifting his weight from back to front with care.

Dennis Quinn was only forty-two years old.

He stopped again at the door to fetch the three pieces of mail from his black letterbox. From which I deduced that he hadn't been outside since early the day before.

I looked past him into the house.

"You saving on electricity?"

"Must look pretty gloomy, huh? I better turn on some lights."

I followed him across the dark foyer through the living room. He and Wendall had used to give their annual mid-winter curry parties here under an eighteenth-century Dutch chandelier of polished brass. We guests would lounge on cushions in front of a high crackling fire with platters of Indian food, and white wine, while a sitar player entertained in the corner. Good food, good music, good friends.

But now that same room was in shadow, lit by a single low watt bulb and layered with dust. The brass chandelier had long since been taken down and sold for medical expenses. The fireplace was cold, holding only dark ashes. There remained the large gilt-edged mirror above it that once had given light and dimension to the room. But tonight it was draped in chintz.

"Thank you for coming, Matt. Last thing I had to sell were our Picasso seriographs. I miss them, but they kept me going three months—You wanted to see the secretary? Right here in the dining room."

The Queen Anne secretary was a museum-quality 1730 piece of burled walnut with undulating, serpentine drawers.

"Wendall had it shipped from England." Dennis said. Then he pulled a chair away from the table and collapsed into it. The walk from the front door here to his dining room had sapped his hourly ration of strength.

"But is was built by Flemish craftsmen," I told him. "The drawers are thicker than we find in British construction."

"It cost ten thousand when we bought it."

"Worth a lot more now."

"Wendall had the eye of an expert. Wouldn't you say?"

"Absolutely." I opened the drawers of the secretary and admired their tight dovetail construction. "An expert."

"In our twenty years together we shopped all over the world looking for just the right items for our home." He wagged a finger. "We had to agree on every single thing. That was our rule."

He reached across the dining room table and touched a framed photograph of himself with Wendall taken in front of The Arc de Triumphe during some youthful summer in Paris. They were laughing and holding up the now departed Picasso seriographs..

Each had been a handsome man in his own way, Wendall being fair and lean while Dennis was dark and sturdily built.

It was hard to see the Dennis of then in the Dennis of now.

"You've made yourselves a beautiful home here."

"It was a real home too, Matt. Not just because of the furniture and the paintings." He held the picture in both trembling hands and gazed at it as though into a mirror. The real ones all having been covered or removed.

"Because we had love. That's the real secret. We were only college boys when we met. But the first time he touched me, we both knew it would be forever. That nothing could part us."

"I know, I.." I tapped the side of the secretary. "Top price would be twenty thousand. But I can offer only fifteen."

"I'll take it."

"Someone else may come in for more."

"Yeah?" He was too weak to snort. "When? Next year?"

"You may want to keep it in your family," I suggested with uttermost tact.

"No family. I appreciate your consideration but I've got no

one at all to leave it to. With Wendall gone."

"If you do get a better offer, we'll cancel this sale." I pulled out my check book.

"Thanks Matt. For everthing."

"I'm making money. The piece may appreciate in value while you're storing it for me."

Some people like Dennis have thousands of dollars invested in artefacts and no cash to pay for their food or medicine. In those cases I agree to buy now and take possession later. ("When they move" is the euphemism we use.) So people like Dennis can continue to enjoy their beautiful things.

Till that time comes when they won't miss them.

"Still you're taking a hell of a chance. What if the house burns down?"

"I'm insured." I handed him the check and the receipt. He leaned on both elbows while he signed it. "The secretary is officially part of my stock now."

"You'll be able to pick it up in a few weeks."

"I'm in no hurry. Believe me. Don't bother to get up; I'll show myself out."

"No. I'll come," He hoisted himself out of his chair, put a claw-like hand on my shoulder, and used me as a crutch all the way to the foyer. "That boy, Raymond?"

"Yes?"

"He was so young, so fine..."

"He was."

"Who'd have believed he would die before I did?"

"I have no answer for that."

Just inside his front door, the famous issue of *Spin* lay on the hall table still folded to the crucial article, the pages now wilted from a hundred turnings, the print all smudged.

Dennis halted and put his palm flat on the issue as though to draw a healing force.

"What do you think of this AL 721?"

"I think... Where there's life there's hope."

He indulged in that thought for no more than a moment before dismissing it with a tired shake of his head.

"No, Matt. I've finally come to the resignation stage of this thing." He slowly rolled up the magazine and dropped it into his brass waste basket where it slid to the bottom with a soft whispering sound.

"I think now I'm ready to meet Wendall."

CHAPTER TWENTY-EIGHT
Sunday Night

Decatur Street looked deserted with only the nightly depopulated wharves and warehouses and the chilly wind coming off the river. It had already seemed hours darker than when I had arrived. As Dennis's light blinked off behind me, I turned right and started down toward Esplanade walking quickly as any city-dweller walks and cautiously, looking around and behind. Not paying enough attention to what was ahead.

The two men were crouching in wait behind a board fence at the corner of Louisa Street. When they sprang out at me, I backed up a step to assess my escape route. But then the smaller of them brandished a precisely-aimed automatic.

"Don'chu even move, Sinclair!"

In the first second I had taken him for a white man as his skin was fair, a strangely opaque shade of pink. But then I saw that his yellow hair was kinky and his face negroid, spotted with large freckles. An albino. His companion was a standard issue dark-skinned black well over six feet tall with a face like a pit bull's.

Both men were dressed in three-piece suits and encumbered with long coats, so I might have been able to outrun them, but not their bullets. I froze in place.

"I don't carry much cash. What do you want?"

"Not cash. We ain't heistmen." The taller thug stepped behind me to clamp my wrists together with his right hand. Then with the left, he grabbed a fistful of forelock and jerked my head back.

The albino was the spokesman. "I got somethin' nice and hard fo' you to suck on, Sinclair." With that, he almost gently insinuated the barrel of his automatic between my lips and past the teeth. He moved it slowly around my tongue. I closed my eyes and tried not to taste the steel and gun oil.

"You comin' fo' a visit. Any objections?" I just closed my eyes and he correctly took that for a heartfelt negative. "But don'chu worry you comin' in high style."

A black Cadillac stretch limousine had been parked on the corner of Louisa and now rolled into sight with its lights off. The driver was a black man in gray livery who looked neither right nor left.

The albino opened the rear door and I didn't put up a graceless struggle as they prodded me inside, pushed me down on the floor and climbed in after me.

There was almost room enough for me to lie full length as the car started up and swung down Decatur Street. The gun remained pointed at my head. Not caring to look up the bore, I stared at the upholstered ceiling instead.

Small talk would have been inappropriate.

After a ten minute drive in light nighttime traffic we reached the Villier Building, at thirty stories one of the tallest in Central Business District. The limousine pulled into the ground floor parking garage and wound up three levels. There was no guard or attendant to cast a look of censure as I was hustled into the private elevator with its single button to the penthouse. Only then did I realize who had choreographed the event.

"This is Nat Ortigue's office."

"Ain't nothin' wrong with you brain." The albino directed me through the sterile hallway and used a key on a door that was undesignated but from the size alone had to belong to the most important office on the floor.

The suite's white carpeting was thick enough to muffle the sound of our footsteps. The furniture was richly upholstered, the wallpaper textured, and the ceiling fitted with accoustic tiles. I surmised that one could scream very loud in this office and not be heard one foot outside of it.

Nat Ortigue himself was alone and standing at the window, his broad back to us. "Leave him here and wait outside," he told my abductors.

He didn't turn around till after they had left us, shutting the door noiselessly behind them. And it was easily seen why he felt no need for body guards.

Ortigue was tall and heavy like a defense lineman who had put on weight in retirement. Back in the fifties, Ortigue had begun his career as an eighteen-year-old boy with no assets but a ruthless ambition and his own muscle. By the age of thirty he had built up a power base among all the black unions along the Gulf Coast. Now he could hire muscle by the ton and never again would be required to rumple his custom-tailored mohair.

"Good evening, Matt." His voice was deep. Tuba deep. "Thank you for coming to see me. I hope you weren't inconvenienced."

He proferred his huge right hand and I noted an onyx ring set with a three-carat diamond solitaire. On him it looked almost dainty.

I let my hand disappear briefly into his. If he wanted to pretend I was there out of courtesy, I would play the game his way.

"I knew it had to be important."

"Most important. I wanted to see you about my man Moses Jones. Good man."

"The best." I could agree without lying. "I've known him since law school."

"Yeah. Have a seat."

Ortigue pointed imperiously to a tufted leather swivel chair then went to sit at his desk, not a desk where any work is actually done but one of those plexiglass ping-pong tables. There was a single stack of computer pages on the blotter.

I sat down like a child in the principal's office, similarly dwarfed by the chair's over-scale.

"I'm a careful son of a bitch, Matt. I ran a complete check on Moses before I invested nearly a quarter of a million of my own money." He put his hand, which would have covered a salad plate, on the stack. "I have the name of the first girl he kissed, his closest buddy in the service and what brand of toothpaste he favored in 1979. No surprises."

"I see."

"Of course I knew about that kid who claimed he was the father of her child. And I knew it was all shee-it."

"Right."

"But evidently that wouldn't have stopped Rodger Lloyd from smearing him with it. Bad dude."

"I see. So did your men make a good dude out of him?"

"No."

"Or of his employee Raymond Harris? He also had that damaging information."

"No way. And that's why I called you in here, Sinclair."

He fixed me with the look of a newly installed African dictator about to execute a political rival. And then eat him.

"It came to me that you were looking in my direction for a suspect. Look elsewhere."

"Right. O.K." I started to hoist myself out of the deep-dish chair. "That's all I needed from you, so I'll be getting along home now..."

"Not like that. You need more convincing."

"Not me, no."

"I've been trying to clear this up for you so we can all get back to a clean campaign. I've put my best men on the investigation but there's nothing out on the street. Nothing."

"I guess you're in a position to know the pimps, the dope dealers, thieves."

"Never said I was Bill Cosby." He picked up the stack of papers and snapped them. "So I conclude that maybe the victims had a personal emeny. Someone could have followed them from Chicago. It had to be a man working on his own because this was *not* a professional hit. You have my word on that."

"I believe you."

"Fine. Then our business is concluded." He pressed the buzzer under his desk and his two thugs appeared like little mechanical figures trotting out of an elaborate German clock.

"Gentlemen? Drive Mr. Sinclair home."

Gratefully, I scrabbled out of my seat. "Do I get to sit up this time?"

"Let him sit up."

CHAPTER TWENTY-NINE

Monday Afternoon

I parked at the wharf without shutting off the engine and let Robin slide over to the wheel. He said, "I'm going to miss you all night."

"It's not my fault you get sea sick." There were steamboat passengers around so he didn't presume to kiss me as I reached in the back seat for my wardrobe bag. "Don't forget to double-lock everything and set the alarms."

Sylvia and her two sons were waiting for me inside the terminal, she shuffling uncomfortably as though afraid of being stood up at the last minute. In a nod to the formality of the occasion, she had at last unbraided her hair which was now dangling in frizzy clumps of black and gray.

Pip saw me as I came through the glass doors and waved.

"Ahoy, uncle! Here we are!"

I caught up to them and took Sylvia's bulging cardboard suitcase from her as we stepped outside to the ramp.

She followed me, shaking her now-free arm. "Aren't you going to wait for a porter or something?"

"I got our keys this morning." I weighed her suitcase in my hand: at least thirty pounds. "But didn't you over-pack for one night?"

"I wanted to have a choice."

I was the first to set foot on deck and inhale the luxurious cruise-ship smell of wood and brass polish. Pip was right behind me, "ah-ing" at the carpeting in the forward cabin lounge.

"The boats on television don't look this rich."

"They're yankee boats. —Right through here. We're on the Chartres Deck."

Once inside Sylvia's cabin, Ronald made a cursory examination of the shower while Pip pulled aside the wooden shutters and examined the stained-glass window panels.

"I expected little round portholes, uncle. These are regular windows."

"All the better to see you with, my dear."

"Sylvia sprung the locks on her suitcase and unfolded two ancient frocks of flowered nylon in Gucci patterns of 1967. One was orange, the other purple.

"Which do you think I would look prettier in?"

I didn't say, "The shower curtain," but just smiled and shook my head in absolute awe of her sense of style.

"This one then." Sylvia shook out the purple travesty. "I'll be a mysterious lady in violet tonight." She bent in front of the dresser mirror to assess her home permanent then put her hands down as though they were no longer of any use. "I did this last night. I was trying for a bouffant but I think I left it on too long. It came out in a fuzzy poodle cut."

"More like a Bassett," Ronald said under his breath.

Sylvia tugged at one of the clumps.

"Matt? Can you help me fix it in time for dinner?"

"We don't *all* do hair, Sylvia."

"Ooh. I'm sorry. I just thought that naturally.."

"I'd better show the boys to their cabin."

Pip, walking beside me through the green carpeted hallway, said, "If this were the Love Boat I'd get to bunk with Jill St. John."

"I didn't see her out there. You'll bunk with your brother and like it."

"But there were some good-looking women back in the terminal. How much time do I have to operate before dinner?"

"Life boat drill is six-thirty. Then you have to be into black tie and at our table by seven."

Ronald carried a canvas duffle bag with Japanese characters across the front. "I won't be late, uncle."

"No," Pip agreed. "*He* won't. All Ronald noticed was this

weird-looking guy who went aboard early. He looked like a white black man."

"An albino," Ronald said.

On reaching our table in the lower deck dining room, I suspected that Pip might have stolen down ahead of time to rearrange the place cards. We were outnumbered three to one by attractive females and Sylvia had somehow been diverted to another table nearer the bandstand.

Throughout, most of the dinner, I was engaged in conversation by a voluptuous blond about my own age (pushing forty). While making all the standard response noises, I amused myself with a house count, categorizing attendees according to their apparent political affiliation. The designer-clad yuppies, white and black, were probably solid for Armand. I pegged the polyester suits with western shirts as Farley Berber's constituents. And of course the unpretentious, overfed blacks among us would be supporting Moses Jones.

The Republican leader, Ollie Dunn, took the microphone to extol Farley's candidacy. A school board member pounded the podium for Moses and my miserable self spoke for Armand. The political speeches were excruciatingly long and boring. Especially mine.

Then the program of New Orleans singers and musicians was too short. As the band leader tooted his last on the clarinet, Pip clapped loudest. "Hey, that's *real* Dixieland Jazz!"

"Perfection," I was happy to agree.

Ronald tapped his glass with a spoon. "The bass was flat on that last number.—Look, there's that albino."

I had to shift to see Ortigue's men, my two abductors, at a rear corner table. The albino saw me the instant I saw him and raised his glass in a mock toast. I did mine.

When the roast beef plates were cleared away, the ladies at our table arose, *en masse*, and migrated to the powder room.

Pip pulled his coffee cup over and started loading it. "Looks like you've made a hit with Vicki."

"Vicki is a bored housewife from Raceland. She and her

girlfriends got the special double room rate and they're looking for a little shipboard romance, à la 'Love Boat'."

"Why not? She's very attractive."

"She's fascinating. But why should such a woman waste her ammunition on me?"

"I get it."

"I'm going to skip dessert and take a turn around the deck." I lowered my voice. "I don't want to hurt her feelings. So will you let the lady know in some subtle manner that I'm not right for her?"

"That you're a three dollar bill?"

"You don't have to put it quite that way."

And with one furtive eye toward the powder room, I made good my escape. I detoured through the forward cocktail lounge where there swayed the usual contingent of cruise drunks who prefer to spend their entire trip on bar stools declaring mutual undying friendship. One such hail fellow waylaid me, hair mussed and tie askew.

"Hey look here, pal. Jus' settle one question for me an' my fren's here. Jus' one lil' ol'.."

"If I can," I stood up perfectly straight to show I wasn't one of them.

He lurched then and threw one arm around my neck for balance.

"Why the hell'd Cher do it?"

"I have no idea."

"Mus' be that new ol' man she's got." He blinked slowly. Sonny never woulda let her."

"Maybe not." I declined a drink, helped him back to his bar stool and sought fresh air.

The program downstairs was still going on in the form of dance music so I thought I would have the deck to myself till I reached the stern.

"Matty? Over here!"

It was Sylvia in her flowered dress, fearfully holding on to the polished teak rail as if for a roller coaster ride. "I've been waiting for you to come out." She looked into the water and then away again quickly. "I'm very scared of the river. It's so black. And aren't there snakes down there?"

"Some."

She looked as though she had seen snakes already. Her eyes were unfocused and she smelled of alcohol.

"Matty, I haven't been straight with you about Rodger Lloyd." The Mississippi breeze butted the clumps of her hair around. "I'm sure this had nothing to do with his murder. But you're entitled to know."

"Know what?"

She gave a sharp coughing laugh and wrung her hands.

"There's someone else I have to talk to first. You dig? I think he should be the first to hear it—But I'll come to your cabin in an hour." And she tottered away along the gently swaying deck clutching at the rail for balance every few feet. The wind blew her dress up high enough to reveal the safety pin holding the lace on her slip.

"If you're still able to move in an hour," I thought.

When I turned back toward the port side I saw a man in a long coat watching me curiously. The albino. When he saw me seeing him, he winked and drifted away.

I didn't have more than a minute to contemplate the black waters in solitude before Pip strolled over to meet me, smiling and breathless.

"I told Vicki the bad news. That you're gay."

"Thank you. I hope she wasn't too disappointed."

"Not at all. Because then I told her the *good* news."

"Which was?"

"That I'm *not*" He raised one well-arched brow and grinned the grin of the invincible. "After all, uncle. I can do anything you can do. More often."

I would like to say he reminded me of myself at that age, but I was never so handsome, so sure.

"Hold on there, Superboy, I'm sure that woman has no interest in a fifteen year old kid."

He leaned against the rail in an unconscious pose like the juvenile in a Noel Coward play. "I told her I was eighteen."

"With no beard?"

"I said we're part Cherokee."

"Don't try that line with an Anthropology major. The Cherokee didn't come this far down the Delta. If we have Indian blood, it's Choctaw."

"I'll remember that for next time."

"You're much too young to be taking up my slack."

"We divvy up. You get all the men on the ship. I take the women. That way we don't cross territories. Fair?"

"I don't have the energy to participate. Better stop off in my cabin and get some raincoats."

"She carries her own. Ribbed, with French ticklers." And he bounded off like a colt in his second spring.

And I wondered if I had ever been that young.

I had retired to my cabin and was shucking my clothes when I heard a light knock on the door. Holding my shirt up to cover my modesty I went to unlock it, assuming that Sylvia had found her way back but instead it was Ronald who stood outside in his robe and pajamas, holding a toothbrush.

"I have to stay in your room tonight."

I was too tired to ask why, so just shrugged and pointed to the other brass bed. He went to the sink and used his toothbrush then fell into bed without another word. I used my own toothbrush and took my nightly dose of dilantin and phenobarbitol. The latter is supposed to carry me past that stage of sleep where seizures occur. It also knocks me right out.

CHAPTER THIRTY
Tuesday Morning

In the morning, the sun awoke me streaming its hot and bright intrusion through the window. The ship was rocking very slightly and grumbling with breakfast noises. I opened one eye and saw Ronald was still there in the next bed. Propped up on one elbow, he studied me owlishly through his thick glasses as though waiting intently for me to wake up.

"I would like to get dressed," he said quietly. "But I'm afraid to barge in on Philip."

I pried myself out of bed. "Afraid? What nonsense." I pulled on my velvet robe, reeled down the hall and knocked a no-nonsense knock on Pip's door. It was opened by Vicki from Raceland, clad only in a bias-cut satin slip which became her. She looked startled at the sight of me then giggled.

"We thought you were room service."

"I couldn't begin to deliver the service that's evidently been going on in this room."

Pip still lounged in the very rumpled bed, his blond hair falling over his brow.

"I was just showing a little Creole hospitality, uncle."

Vicki rooted around for her dress before finding it at last in a heap by the bathroom door.

"This nephew of yours is young. But you know I didn't have to teach him anything.—Except that Cherokees weren't indigenous to this part of the delta."

Pip shrugged. "Slip of the tongue. I meant Choctaw."

Vicki squirmed into her low-cut silk jacquard evening dress.

"I hate dragging back upstairs to my cabin in this get-up. What will people think?"

The breakfast seating in the dining room was poorly attended, as most revelers were still pretending it wasn't tomorrow and were drinking theirs in the forward cocktail lounge.

My teetotling nephews and I were already into our omelettes when the Republican, Ollie Dunn, came down the stairs conspicuously alone. He had brought a newspaper for company.

I called him to join us. "Welcome to Tuesday, Ollie. How come you're not upstairs drinking with the money men."

He lay his *Times-Picayune* alongside his napkin.

"I can't drink. I'm an alcoholic."

"Really? I've always wondered why drunks never admit they're alcoholics. Only reformed drunks do."

"Because admitting it is taking responsibility for it.—Those Eggs Benedict look good. Where's the rest of your party? The lady."

"I don't know. I expected Sylvia to join us for breakfast."

Ronald didn't look up from his omelette. "Mom doesn't always eat breakfast. Maybe she's just having some toaster pastries in her cabin."

Pip jumped to his feet. "I'll go ask her if she wants anything. Be back in a few minutes."

Ollie opened his newspaper. "Excuse my rudeness. I've just got to find out."

"Find out how we're doing in the polls?"

"No, find out if the Saints are being blacked out this week. For the first time in fifteen years, I can attend home games without my paper bag."

"The NFL strike gave us the best season we ever had," Ronald said. "Those replacements believe in winning."

"I'll be sorry to see 'em go. Especially John Fourcade."

"Oh, they're keeping Fourcade."

"I say keep them all. We may make the play-offs."

"That'll be a long-overdue miracle. Up till now, we've always had the shortest season in the league."

Ronald nodded grimly. "We probably don't even have the

technology to *print* play-off tickets."

Vicki from Raceland appeared in the doorway, cast around uncertainly till she saw our table, then in the space of two seconds smiled and frowned. She covered her disappointment and joined us anyway.

"Hi, Matt. Where's uh...?"

"He'll be back in a minute."

"Oh." She took the chair beside Pip's cooling plate.

Vicki looked demure and matronly now in her cotton shirtwaist. But there was still a tell-tale glow in her cheeks.

"I just wanted to say bye-bye before we disembark."

"He went back to the cabin deck to find his mother."

"Sylvia? She's sort of... odd."

"You must have met her."

"Not exactly. She came to the cabin."

"Philip's?"

"Yes, and when she knocked on the door, well I was.. indisposed. So I had to run and hide in the bathroom but no more than a minute. I could hear her through the door.."

"Sounding odd?"

"Sort of whiney, you know? Then she left and Philip told me she was just trying to find Ronald."

"Oh? Did she find you, Ronald?"

"Nope." He was reading the comic section.

I sneaked a glance at Garfield before turning back to Vicki.

"Did you run into Sylvia later?"

"No, we never left the room. Not till you interrupted us this morning."

"Sorry."

Ollie's eyebrows went up. Perhaps in response to an editorial about the city sales tax.

Like any sexually excited woman, Vicki was always eager to tell more than anyone should hear. She leaned across Pip's chair and whispered. "That handsome nephew of yours is marvelous. What stamina!"

"Ah.." I was watching Ollie's eyebrows. "I'm sure."

"We did it three times."

"Very strenuous, I should imagine."

"No kidding. We both conked out and slept like logs."

Ollie smiled and handed me the Vivant section. "Say, Matt. Would you like to read Dear Abby?"

Sensible Dear Abby. "I think I'd better."

By the time Pip rejoined us, his omelette had chilled. He reclaimed his chair next to Vicki, casually resting a proprietary hand on her knee as though he were a slightly jaded man of the world and she his mistress of long standing.

"Mother wasn't in her cabin," he said. "But she left her purse on the bed. So I tried the upper deck, the cabin deck, the forward cocktail lounge... I even asked a stewardess to check the Ladies' lounge, Where could she have gone?"

Ronald didn't look up from the Sports section.

"Where can you go on a ship?"

"Where?" Suddenly I had a recollection of Sylvia tottering along the brass and teak rail, the wind blowing her dress up. "We'd better spread out and comb every deck. I'm going to ask the captain to put out an all-points."

Forty-five minutes later, I met the ship's captain midway along the top deck. "I'm sorry, Mr. Sinclair." he said. "We have searched every corner of this ship large enough to hold a human being. Your cousin is nowhere to be found."

"She couldn't have fallen overboard. Considering the height of this rail."

"I agree. Is it possible that she jumped?"

"No."

"Then.." He held his palms out. "Suppose she was pushed."

Ronald had walked up so quietly that I hadn't heard him. But now he stood holding Sylvia's purse in one hand and an open letter in the other. The envelope was unstamped and addressed simply to "Rodger".

CHAPTER THIRTY-ONE
Thursday Morning

Two days after Sylvia's body was found washed up on a sand bar close to Myrtle Grove. I brought my nephews some groceries.

The house on Banks was quiet when Pip met me at the door. Sinclairs don't cry, of course, but he looked pale and haggard as he hugged me tightly.

"I'll miss her so much. What will we all do without her?"

I patted his shoulder. What do you tell a boy who has just lost the most important person in his life?

"I'm sorry," was all that came out. "I've brought some food. I didn't think you would have time to cook."

We went back to the kitchen table where Sylvia had spent so many hours of her day, years of her life, drinking boiled instant Maxwell House, reading tabloids, and smoking plants from the window box.

Pip said, "I couldn't eat anything now, uncle."

"You'll have to force down something. With your father um... 'away', you boys will have to make the vigil yourselves tomorrow night."

I could see Ronald through the open door of his room, bent over his computer. Business as usual.

When I stepped in to offer condolences, he didn't look up.

"I'm trying to find out what year Rodger Lloyd taught at Tulane."

"He's been obsessed with that," Pip offered. "Mother's letter said one of us is Lloyd's son, and Ronald won't sleep till he knows which."

"It hardly matters," I said lightly.

"If my father isn't really my father, it matters." Ronald rubbed his eyes under his glasses which were so smudged I wondered that he could see through them at all. "I've finally tapped into Tulane's central data bank. They have records dating back to 1965 but only for certain departments."

I said, "As an officer of the court, I have to tell you that hacking is against the law."

"Yeah, I know. I'll print it out before they catch us." This consideration was of little moment. "What I had to do was conduct a name search. Rodger Lloyd." He pressed some buttons. "See? The only man by that name ever to be associated with Tulane. Thank God it wasn't Jim Johnson or Hank Brown." The numbers rolled down the monitor and Ronald pressed the space key to halt them. "You see? Here it is. Professor Lloyd was mentioned in the yearbook for the school year ending June nineteen-seventy but he seemed to have been issued a lecturer's fee in the spring of seventy-two."

Pip's eyes were wide. "So?"

"So, count on your fingers, dolt. Any child conceived during that first period would be sixteen, my age today. During the second period, he would be fifteen, your age. I'll make hard copy." He pushed more buttons and a minute later the data began clattering through the dot matrix printer across the room.

"That's inconclusive," I said.

"Yes. So next thing I checked was father's Service record. He could have begot me just before he left for Viet Nam, assuming I wasn't premature. Then he came home on leave for thirty days between tours, so he could have made mother pregnant with you."

"Still nothing concrete."

The clattering noise of the printer stopped suddenly and turned into a shriek.

Pip covered his ears. "It's broken down."

"No, when it whistles in F sharp like that, it just means the ribbon needs changing." Ronald wheeled over to the printer and pulled the ribbon out. The noise stopped. "I've got plenty more."

I sat down on the bed, hard. "Pip, will you get my briefcase out of the trunk." I handed him the car keys and he looked puzzled but moved to obey without an argument.

Ronald turned his chair around to face me.

"Do you have something to input."

"An article in *Bird Watcher's Digest* written by Rodger Lloyd. I think you'll find it informative."

CHAPTER THIRTY-TWO

Thursday Evening

I wasn't home long enough to take off my coat when Frank Washington rang.

"Guess what, Matt? Your cousin George wants to see you down at the lock-up right away."

"Really? I thought he had disowned me. Something about a sissy gay.."

"'Pantiwaist fag' was how he put it."

"Thank you."

"But he must have softened in his hour of grief. Will you talk to him?"

"I shall."

The difference between "shall" and "will" is the matter of futurity versus volition. I *shall* pay my taxes. (Not wanting to but it's inevitable.) I *will* eat turtle sauce piquante for dinner. (Very much wanting to.)

As I'm an attorney we didn't have to meet in the visitor's room with a screen between us, but were shown into cubicle big enough for a table and two wooden chairs. George was wearing green prison issue coveralls with the initials "OPP" in white across the back but showed excellent spirits for a new widower. He looked, in fact, happier than I'd seen him in years, grinning and shaking my hand vigorously as we took our seats.

"Hi, cousin. Thanks so much for coming down."

"No problem. Are you going to let me help you?"

"That's not why I called in you here. I don't want favors."

"I wouldn't consider it so. Your original bail was revoked, but I think I can arrange…"

"That won't be necessary now. You see, I have solid alibis for the times when Lloyd and Harris were killed."

"Someone saw you fishing?"

"Fishing?" He snorted then as though he were dealing with an idiot. "I never even wet a line. That was just the story I gave Sylvia every Saturday."

"All right. Let's have the true version."

"Can't you guess? I was with a woman during both time periods. And she'll testify to it."

"Name?"

"I can tell you now. Her name is Emily Gilcrest and she waits tables at Bailey's. We've been seeing each other for two years."

"That's not going to look good, George. If the woman loves you, she'll be happy to charge in here and declare that you were in bed with her all day and night. Who will believe her?"

He smiled like a man holding the Ace of Trumps. "But we weren't in bed. You see, Emily and I took her six year old daughter, Annie, to the Muppets Ice Show. It was an unforgettable experience for all of us. The little girl saved the programs and the ticket stubs."

I tried not to sound like "Church Lady". "How convenient."

"We spend every spare moment together. Emily and I are very much in love and have been for a long time."

"Congratulations. But when you got yourself arrested for murder, why didn't 'very much in love' come forward to exonerate you."

"And let the whole world know we'd been having an affair?—I couldn't let Sylvia find out."

"You were afraid she would leave you."

"Not that. I hadn't had anything with my wife for years. But I'm sure she would have done something dangerous."

"Dangerous?"

"You knew Sylvia, Matt. The woman was subject to enormous depressions. She had tried suicide several times already. If she'd found out about Emily, that would have pushed her over the edge for good."

"They say something did."

"But not us. We were very discreet. I was even willing to stay in jail to save my wife's feelings. Doesn't that mean something?"

"That you're incredibly stupid."

"I thought I only had to stick it out till the police found the real murderer."

"Don't be naive. They stopped looking for the real murderer after they'd got you."

"But I was in no real danger, Matt. Since I didn't kill Lloyd, how could anyone have proved I did?"

"A good prosecutor with political ambitions arguing against an underpaid, overworked public defender in front of a crime-ridden urban jury could convict Santa Claus of the Zodiac Murders."

"If the case against me got to looking really bad, Emily would have testified, of course."

"The longer she waited, the harder it would be to prove the story wasn't concocted."

"I know that. But we don't have to worry about Sylvia anymore. So tomorrow, Emily and her little girl are coming in to give their statements."

"That may not be enough to spring you but it'll be considered. I'll talk to the D.A."

"And I'll be back home with the boys by the weekend. This whole nightmare is finally over."

"Not by half. We still have to know who murdered Rodger Lloyd with your fishing knife."

"Hey, anyone can reach in the back of a pick-up truck." His eyes shifted. "Must have been some black punk."

"Some black punk would not have been invited to Lloyd's hotel room for drinks."

"Matt.." George strained as though laboring with the truth. "That's why I thought maybe it was Sylvia. She was crazy. I mean it wasn't her fault. But do you think she might have lost her reason and killed that guy?"

"And then killed herself?"

"Who else?"

CHAPTER THIRTY-THREE

Election Day

"Look! It's raining!"

Steve screwed up his face. "You didn't need to walk in here with a weather report, Matt. It's been that way all day. Hell, I was out *in* the damn stuff."

I folded my dripping umbrella and dropped it into the copper stand by the door. "But don't you know what it means? God is a moderate!"

"Oh, I see what you're driving at." Steve perched on the arm of a tufted leather desk chair. "The poor people are staying home in droves."

"They don't have cars. They don't even have rain coats!"

"You find that very amusing."

"Surely they won't risk bringing their precious little children out in the rain to slog down to the polls."

"And vote for Moses Jones."

"Voter apathy. I *love* it. Karen and I have been celebrating all afternoon."

"Don't get out the funny hats yet. The polls won't close for three more hours."

"By then I'll be watching the thrilling results with Pip, over at his house."

"Why over there? His father will be let out tomorrow." Steve looked serious. "And Armand's people are all getting together at the Roosevelt to wait for the returns."

"I have another agenda."

In the kitchen on Banks Street, Pip put a bowl of hot popcorn in front of me and adjusted the counter TV set.

"Ronald will be sorry he missed this. But he thought some

judo match in Baton Rouge was more important than the election."

Warren was on screen somberly reporting the early returns.

"Armand Voitier is well in the lead with 42% of the vote." Armand's name blinked and changed color on the tote board. "And we project that he will keep that lead."

"Yayy!" Pip waved a fistful of popcorn.

"And Moses Jones has edged ahead of Farley Berber for second place," Warren announced.

"I knew it," I said. "It was pre-ordained with the weather report."

"I wish we could spend more evenings like this. But my father's coming home tomorrow." Pip sighed deeply. "It'll be back to business as usual."

"Nothing will be usual till Lloyd's murderer is found."

"You said they don't have grounds to hold my father."

"No, they heard the suspect's witnesses and believed them. But it's time now to mind the victim's witness."

My nephew laughed hollowly. "There wasn't one."

"There was the silent witness. Lloyd's book of bird illustrations."

Pip dug into the popcorn. "That warbler picture?"

"Not the warbler. The victim was pointing to the cuckoo on the facing page."

He smiled puckishly. "Did Lloyd know someone named cuckoo?"

"The clue wasn't in the name but in a unique behavior pattern of the genus. What they call brood parasitism."

He cocked his head very slightly. "What's that?"

When a cuckoo lays an egg, she doesn't stay around to hatch it herself. Instead she sneaks it into the nest of another bird, say a wren. Then the unknown wrens hatch a little cuckoo."

"Sort of a foster child." He pushed the popcorn over to me and I shook my head.

"There's a more sinister implication. You see, cuckoos are

quite a lot bigger than wrens. So when the cuckoo hatches, he pushes the baby wrens out of the nest so he can grab all the worms for himself."

"And what happens to the baby wrens?"

"They die. If they didn't, the cuckoo wouldn't get enough to eat and *he* would die."

Pip lifted his chin. "It seems cruel. But there's nature, isn't it? The survival of the stongest?"

"I finally realized what Lloyd was trying to say with his dying message. He meant 'the cuckoo in the nest'. The false heir."

"What's that?"

"He meant you, Pip."

My nephew tightened his fist around the popcorn and it crackled.

"Hey, that's off the wall."

"Lloyd told Raymond Harris that he'd seen his son. He probably approached you the next day to introduce himself. He might even have thought you would be happy to meet him."

Pip set his lips grimly. "He was." He opened his hand and let the popcorn fall out. "The fool thought he could step in here and rob me of my name and everything that goes with it. Rodger Lloyd actually admitted he was broke and had nothing to offer. *Nothing.* As his son, I would have nothing."

"You didn't say that though. You pretended to accept him as your father so you could get into his hotel room and kill him."

He shook his head. "No, that wasn't me. You forget I give lessons every Saturday."

"Your story fell apart when I realized it had rained so much that morning that the park was mud soup. Karen confirmed that lessons had to be cancelled."

"You were stupid not to check that earlier."

"Blind and stupid. You lifted your father's fishing knife."

Pip got to his feet and looked down at me. "I'd known about Emily Gilcrest for months. I knew where Dad parked is pick-up every Saturday and also that he wouldn't be using the fishing gear himself."

"So you had an easily concealed murder weapon. Tell me. Would you have let George go to Angola for a murder you had committed?"

"In a New York second. Dad was a loser and a liability. All he ever did was try to get between you and me."

"Is that a compliment?"

"You were the essential Sinclair, uncle, and everything I wanted to be." Then he frowned suddenly. "Well, I never wanted to be queer of course, but all the rest of it. Rich, powerful, respected... You lived the way I wanted to. It was my birthright."

"There's no such thing as a birthright."

Pip looked unsure for a bare moment. "Just as a matter of interest, how did you know it was me? Ronald could have been the false heir."

"Your brother's alibi is unimpeachable. His Source bill confirms that he was logged into the computer library at the time Rodger Lloyd was murdered."

He moved picked up his book bag. "That was all?"

"I considered something else. You never met Raymond Harris."

"Thank God. You've been decent enough to keep that side of your life to yourself."

"Yet Sylvia told me you had collapsed when you heard about his murder on the news."

"It could have been you."

"But Frank Washington said my name hadn't been released for the six o'clock news. So how did you know I was even acquainted with Harris?"

He pulled out a stack of text books. "That was a mistake."

"Undoubtedly. You saw Raymond and me through the window."

"I did." His eyes flashed. "Kissing like a couple of queers."

"But why did you kill him?"

"That was a mistake. Before we went to Texas, I heard you and Steve talking about Robin. You were going to deed over half your house to that little pansy."

"That was cause for murder?"

He sounded cool and clinical, not insane. "First I tried to take you out before you signed the papers."

"By setting me up with the loco horse."

"But you're too good a rider, uncle. So after you signed the papers, I had to rip off Dad's target pistol and go after Robin."

"And through the window in the dark, you thought Raymond was him."

"The mansion of St. Charles was my inheritance. You promised it to me!"

"You heard only the last part of the conversation, Pip. It wasn't the old Sinclair family home I was giving, just the house we live in on Esplanade."

"So I killed the wrong man and for the wrong reason. The joke was on me." He reached into his book bag again and brought out a particularly nasty-looking .38 revolver.

I tried not to flinch. "Your father's missing pistol. They searched every inch of the house for that."

"But not Mrs. Boudreaux's locker at the stables." He twirled it around his finger. "Guess what? It's loaded."

"I don't doubt it. What happens now?"

The barrel was pointing at my chest and never wavered.

"What's wrong gets right."

He opened the kitchen drawer without looking and felt around for a roll of black electrical tape. "There was only one advantage to having a shop teacher for a father. I learned how to improvise." Without lowering his gun, he lifted the tape and unrolled a foot of it with his teeth. "Turn around and put your hands behind your back." I did as he said and he wrapped the tape around my wrists. "Then Karen had to be fixed."

"Why her?"

"You think I'm stupid, uncle? I know what a home pregnancy test looks like. It was sitting right on her desk. The ring was unmistakable."

"You thought she was carrying my child?"

"Once you had a kid of your own, I'd be history. But I fixed it so there was no kid."

"How did you get into the costume party?"

"Karen's invitation was on her desk at the stable."

"Now I remember her saying she misplaced it."

"I had no trouble getting through the gate in jeans, a sweat-shirt and a Ronald Reagan mask. I saw you buy the drinks." With a firm hand on my shoulder, he pushed me into Sylvia's chair. "This is necessary. You'll understand." He unrolled more tape and wrapped it around my throat and to the back of the chair winding it several times.

I was barely able to speak.

"Why did you kill your mother?"

"You know that too?"

"Vicki's saying you had made love to her three times sounded like an all-night alibi till I remembered that when I was your age, I could do it three times in fifteen minutes."

"I satisfied her."

"You exhausted her. Then while she was asleep you went out to meet your mother."

He reached back into the drawer without taking his gun off me and produced an extension cord and a palm-sized electrical device. "This is a rheostat." He placed the gun on his knee and used a kitchen knife to cut the extension cord in half. Then he cut the socket off and carefully stripped the wires while he talked. "I heard your conversation on deck, that's why. She was going to tell you about me."

"That you were Rodger Lloyd's son?"

"She was the only person who knew. Still living."

"It was all for my money then."

"Mother was a totally useless person. No one will miss her." He whistled tunelessly while attaching two cut ends of the extension cord to the rheostat.

I tried to move but the tape choked me. "What about me?"

"Oh, they'll miss you. *I'll* miss you."

"You think you can get away with murder again?"

"Not murder, uncle. You're going to die of *natural* causes."

"Here in your kitchen?"

"They gave my mother shock treatments at Pineville. You

understand the principle."

"Electricity through the brain. An artificially induced epileptic seizure."

"Exactly." He reached into his book bag for his walkman and detached the headphones. "You've been having them all your life." He taped the cut ends of the wire to the ear pieces and carefully arranged the rig on my head. I could feel the exposed wires pricking my scalp through the hair. "No one will guess it wasn't just one of your regular fits unless they shave your head to find the burn marks."

"Don't try it Pip, there's something you don't know."

"Damn, uncle!" He snatched up a dish towel, pulled my head back and stuffed the limp cotton rag in my mouth. "I respect you so much now. Don't wreck it at the last minute by pleading!" He tore off another foot of electrical tape and secured the gag. "You'll only be inconvenienced a little while. I don't intend for there to be any pain. I don't want to hurt you; you've always been good to me." He kissed my cheek, as softly as a woman does because he had no beard. A baby-faced murderer.

"There's no malice, uncle. If I had ever loved anyone, it would have been you." He placed the rheostat on a chair and plugged in the jerry-rigged cord. "I'll start the current low and dial it up gradually to induce the convulsions without electricuting you. You will just have seizures until you stop breathing. Who would question it?"

He bent over to dial up the rheostat and I felt a faint bussing on my scalp.

Then the collision happened. And in the next milli-second the buzzing ceased as the deadly wire had torn loose when Pip was knocked sprawling to the floor with his brother Ronald on top of him.

When Ronald sprang to his feet again the pistol was in his hand, unfired.

"Are you all right, uncle?"

As he ripped the lethal headset off me, I was looking past him to where Pip had fallen across the two live wires. I tried to communicate but could make no sound.

"Don't worry, I've disarmed him." Ronald reached for the tape around my throat instead of the gag and began unwinding it carefully. "I'm sorry I'm late. I waited outside according to plan till he gave himself away. There'd have been no problem taking him unarmed." He worked with maddening slowness. "But then I saw the gun through the window and knew I had to get in without making any noise. I stood right there on the other side of the door till he was distracted."

I watched Philip's fair young body jerk with the current, no less horrified for knowing he felt nothing. It was like seeing myself die.

"Why do you look so scared, uncle? It's all over now." Ronald finished unwinding then picked up Pip's serrated knife to cut my wrists free at last.

I tore off my gag and pointed. "Get him!"

Ronald turned around then to see his brother lying with eyes open and back arched, shaking in rhythmic vibration. He stepped deliberately over to the wall outlet and pulled the plug. The shaking stopped.

Ronald looked down and shook his head. "Sorry, it's no good."

"Dead?"

"The wire snapped back and hit him in the face so the juice went right through his brain." he reported as though describing a chemical chain reaction. "He's gone."

"But there might still be a chance! Do you know CPR?"

Ronald remained impassive. "No sir, I don't."

I was at the phone before he finished saying it and punched 911. I was too frantic to remember the address and Ronald supplied it calmly.

The receiver shook as I replaced it on the cradle.

"They'll be here in a few minutes. They're good."

"I know." Ronald put his hands on my shoulders. "Listen. We agreed we would finish this tonight."

My head hurt. "Sinclair family business. We had to take care of it ourselves."

"So let's get our story straight: this was a simple accident. I was in there working on my computer and Philip phoned you to say he was trying some new experiment." He stated this fabrication in a flat tone. "You thought it sounded dangerous and wanted to stop him. But by the time you got here, he was dead. A tragic mistake. That's all."

The boy was right and I said so. Why should anyone else have to know a Sinclair was capable of cold-blooded murder.

The real Sinclair.

"Sit down, uncle." Ronald gently pushed me back into the chair. He pulled another chair over, deliberately positioned it to block my view of Pip, and sank down beside me.

"I know you loved him. But remember he was a born murderer. As you said, a sociopath."

"The seed of Ernest Sinclair."

"He would have killed you like he did your friend Raymond, and my mother. And my father."

"It was all due to Rodger Lloyd's fatal mistake," I said. "Sylvia wouldn't tell him his son's name so he knew only that the older of the two boys was his."

"Then he tracked us down to the school yard."

"When a man sees two brothers together, it's natural to assume that the taller one is the older."

Ronald pushed his glasses up. "And if you're a man with normal pride, you would presume that the fairer, stronger, more handsome one is your own."

"So he approached Pip instead of you, and introduced himself as his true father."

"And my greedy and snobbish little brother just saw his Sinclair birthright slipping away from him, the money and the name,. So he couldn't let Lloyd tell his story."

"If only he'd waited to learn the truth."

"You could have told him, uncle."

"Not right away. Lloyd is a Welsh name but it took me time to connect that the man had a genetic gift peculiar to the Welsh."

Ronald nodded, not looking up. "Perfect pitch."

"His magazine article described the notes in a bird's song. And when you said your printer was shrieking in high F sharp, I knew you had the same gift."

"I've always taken it for granted. Never gave a thought to where it came from until you pointed it out to me." He swallowed hard. "Of course those things are inherited."

"Not from our side of the family, and Sylvia couldn't carry a tune at all."

He studied his hands. "I'm sorry I never met Rodger Lloyd. But the thing I most regret is that I'm not a Sinclair after all."

"But you are."

"I mean really."

"Really." We heard the siren of the paramedics coming. Fast but too late. "Ronald, you must be my nephew. Everyone who knew otherwise is dead. Besides you're all I've got now."

He frowned and shook his head. "I can't take his place for you. I'll never be tall and handsome and charming like my brother."

"But.." I repeated slowly. "You're all I've got."

He studied my face then and believed me.

"Good enough, uncle."

That settled, he put his arm around my neck and hugged me. Some people might have taken this for a highly emotional moment, but of course we didn't cry.

Sinclairs don't.